WITHDRAWN
FROM
COLLECTION

D0405806

MR
CADMUS

Also by Peter Ackroyd

FICTION

The Great Fire of London
The Last Testament of Oscar Wilde
Hawksmoor
Chatterton
First Light
English Music
The House of Doctor Dee
Dan Leno and the Limehouse
Golem
Milton in America

The Plato Papers
The Mystery of Charles Dickens
The Clerkenwell Tales
The Lambs of London
The Fall of Troy
The Casebook of Victor Frankenstein
The Canterbury Tales – A Retelling
The Death of King Arthur: The
Immortal Legend – A Retelling
Three Brothers

NON-FICTION

Notes for a New Culture: An Essay
on Modernism
Dressing Up: Transvestism and Drag,
the History of an Obsession
Ezra Pound and His World
T. S. Eliot
Dickens' London: An Imaginative
Vision
Ezra Pound and his World (1989)
Dickens
Introduction to Dickens
Blake
The Life of Thomas More
London: The Biography
The Collection: Journalism, Reviews,
Essays, Short Stories, Lectures
Dickens: Public Life and Private
Passion
Albion: The Origins of the English
Imagination
The Beginning
Illustrated London
Escape From Earth
Ancient Egypt
Chaucer (Penguin Classics' "Brief
Lives" series)
Shakespeare: The Biography
Ancient Greece

Ancient Rome
Turner Brief Lives
Thames: Sacred River
Coffee with Dickens
(with Paul Schlicke)
Newton (Penguin Classics'
"Brief Lives" series)
Poe: A Life Cut Short
Venice: Pure City
The English Ghost
London Under
The History of England,
v.1 Foundation
Wilkie Collins (Penguin Classics'
"Brief Lives" series)
The History of England, v.2 Tudors
The History of England, v.3 Civil
War (also available as Rebellion:
The History of England from James
I to the Glorious Revolution)
Charlie Chaplin
Alfred Hitchcock
The History of England,
v.4 Revolution
Queer City
The History of England,
v.5 Dominion

MR
CADMUS

PETER
ACKROYD

CANONGATE

First published in Great Britain in 2020 by Canongate Books Ltd,
14 High Street, Edinburgh EH1 1TE

canongate.co.uk

2

Copyright © Peter Ackroyd, 2020

The right of Peter Ackroyd to be identified as the
author of this work has been asserted by him in accordance
with the Copyright, Designs and Patents Act 1988

British Library Cataloguing-in-Publication Data
A catalogue record for this book is available on
request from the British Library

ISBN 978 1 78689 894 4

Typeset in Bembo by
Palimpsest Book Production Ltd, Falkirk, Stirlingshire

Printed and bound in Great Britain by Clays Ltd, Elcograf S.p.A.

MIX
Paper from
responsible sources
FSC
www.fsc.org FSC® C018072

Chapter 1

The Yellow Car

The three cottages stood in a row at the eastern end of Little Camborne. They had once been owned by three families who worked the land of the local squire, but the badly dressed stone of the eighteenth century had been restored and replastered. They were now painted white, and the thatch had given way to tiles.

The first of them – 1, The Coppice – was owned by Maud Finch. At the age of fifty-five Miss Finch still held herself erect; she had firm opinions and a firm manner of expressing them. She wore rather severe clothes and from a distance might have been mistaken for either sex. Millicent Swallow lived at 3, The Coppice. Miss Swallow was a mild and complaisant woman; she was younger than Miss Finch, and was described by her neighbour as 'a little vague around the edges'. She had wispy hair and her eyes watered in the wind; she favoured silk blouses and cashmere scarves, but she always looked as if her clothes had been put on in a hurry. In this respect she was perfectly unlike her neighbour, who dressed with what she believed to be finesse. How they had struck so firm a friendship was one of the small mysteries of Little Camborne.

The cottage that stood between them had been vacant for over three months. Its previous occupant had been a retired schoolmaster, Mr Herrick, who had soon become something of an irritant to both ladies. He played Chopin too loudly on the gramophone, and the offensive smoke from his pipe drifted over their garden fences. So the ladies were not displeased when he died suddenly of heart failure. Now they contemplated the fate of the empty cottage. 'I hope it's not people from London,' Miss Swallow remarked nervously on the day after the funeral.

'Or a family.'

'Surely it's not big enough for a family?'

'You never know. Some of them live like pigs.'

A few prospective purchasers had visited the cottage, in the company of the agent, and one or other of the ladies managed to busy herself in her front garden as they left. 'It is a lovely little property,' the agent would say. 'Quite bijou.'

'What does that mean?' Miss Swallow asked Miss Finch on the first occasion she heard it.

'It is French.' That seemed to satisfy both of them. The likely purchasers were, in Miss Finch's opinion, all 'ghastly'. A retired couple from Barnes were considered to be common, while two young men arriving in a smart sports-car were treated with great suspicion. 'Don't say *anything*,' Miss Finch told her.

'But you see them on television all the time.'

'That doesn't make it *right*.'

When the agent brought with him a single man, in his early forties, Miss Swallow was greatly relieved. 'I know a gentleman when I see one,' she said to her neighbour. 'Very much of the old school.'

'Too good to be true. The estate agent tells me that he is working for a foreign client.'

'A *foreign* client? Oh my goodness.'

It was with some trepidation, therefore, that, two weeks later, they watched a large removal van draw up before the cottages. Both of them looked out of their windows at the same moment, but nothing happened. A few minutes later a small yellow car appeared around the bend of the dusty road, and came to a halt behind the van. Out of it jumped a man wearing green trousers and a scarlet sweater, with a plaid scarf tied loosely around his neck. 'This,' Miss Finch said to herself, 'is the foreigner.'

Two men in green overalls now alighted from the van as the foreign gentleman opened the gate to the middle cottage and scampered up the path of the front garden. 'Oh, this is excellent. Too excellent for words.' He turned to the two men. 'Well, my friends, what do you think of my lovely English cottage? Is it not enchanting?' He put his hands to his lips, and blew it a kiss. 'You are irresistible. Highly irresistible.'

Miss Finch noted that he had a slightly swarthy complexion, with a pencil-thin moustache. He was perhaps in his late fifties, of middle height, and seemed to her to resemble a mature Douglas Fairbanks. Miss Swallow, on the other hand, saw in him a likeness to William Holden, whom she had watched in *The Towering Inferno* some years before.

He caught sight of her before she had time to move away from her window, and he put out his arms. 'Oh, my good English neighbour! I hope you will make me welcome!' She did not know quite what to do, but she waved her hand in a timid greeting. To her acute embarrassment he blew a kiss to her. Miss Finch, half-hidden by a large vase of lilies on her window ledge, drew in her breath. She could not see what

Miss Swallow was doing, but she hoped that she was not encouraging him. She now stepped out so that she was in full view, and he noticed the movement. 'Oh, I am blessed,' he said. 'Two lovely ladies on my doorstep!' He did not blow her a kiss, but put his hand upon his heart; or at least upon the relevant part of his scarlet jumper.

The two removal men had opened the back of the van, and with a flourish of his keys the new neighbour hastened into the cottage. The two ladies now pressed more eagerly against their windows. A small piano came out, followed by a wooden chest and a sideboard of polished mahogany. A single bed then emerged, as well as a divan and a dining-room table. Rolled carpets, lamps, and what looked suspiciously like tapestries, were carried into the cottage. Miss Finch could hear him singing what she took to be a Italian medley in a strong baritone voice. And what was this? A large and empty parrot cage. Several suitcases were then taken inside together with stools, chairs and leather pouffes. Some ornate candelabra were the last to leave the van.

Miss Swallow felt quite exhausted by all the activity. She sat down in her favourite armchair, covered in faded green silk. She did not think she had the strength to make herself a cup of tea. She dared not leave the house, in case *he* should emerge, but she desperately wanted to consult with Miss Finch. So she called her on the telephone.

'Maud, what an extraordinary way to behave!'

'Did you see his car? It is so yellow.'

'But all that kissing and screaming—'

'I don't think he screamed, dear,' Maud told her. 'But he was loud.'

'What are we to make of him?'

'We will have to wait and see. He was singing Italian songs, by the way.'

'Is that where he's from?'

'I haven't the faintest idea. Even before he opened his mouth, I knew he was foreign.'

'Oh dear. I hope he doesn't have any habits.'

'Such as what?'

'You know. Food and so forth. And late hours.'

'I saw a parrot cage but no parrot.'

'It will be in quarantine. Birds carry the most terrifying diseases.'

'If it squawks, I shall complain. And what about that piano? Sound carries a long way out here.'

'I really don't know what to do.' Miss Swallow was now thoroughly alarmed at vistas of parrots and pianos.

'We must stay strong, Millicent.'

Early that evening the doorbell to Miss Swallow's cottage chimed. It was the foreigner. He was standing on the threshold, with a box of chocolates in his hand.

'Ah, do I intrude?'

'Not at all.'

'Mr Cadmus. Theodore Cadmus. Theo.'

'Miss Swallow.' She put out her hand to avoid being kissed. 'These are for you, dear lady. The smallest possible token—'

'Oh, that is too kind, really.'

'May I?'

'Yes,' she added, with a hint of nervousness. 'Do. Come in.'

He inched his way along the hallway into the front parlour. 'Oh, this is delightful. What sweet ornaments and bouquets.' Miss Swallow had a taste for chintz and porcelain. 'And who is this gorgeous creature?'

'Timothy.'

He picked up the marmalade cat and, much to the animal's discomfiture, kissed it on its nose. 'Extra special.'

'May I offer you a glass of sherry, Mr Cadmus? Or wine perhaps?'

'We will drink our fill of golden sunshine. One of your national poets tells us this.'

'I'm afraid I only have a Beaujolais from Tesco. Or a Moselle.'

'I am at your disposal.' The cat, showing signs of struggle, was put down. 'The red and the white are for me equally delicious.'

So she brought out the Beaujolais, on the very sound principle that the bottle was unopened, and made a good impression on her visitor. She suggested a chair. She did not know quite what to say to him. 'Will you be with us long?'

'Oh, an eternity. I have come to stay. After a storm-tossed life I am come into harbour.' *Whatever could he mean? Storm-tossed? It sounded rather exciting.*

'Where do you come from, Mr Cadmus?' She only just remembered his name. 'If I may ask?'

'My very good lady, I come from a small island in the Mediterranean. It will mean nothing to you.'

'I suppose not.'

'We are small. We are under two hundred persons.'

'Rather like Little Camborne.'

'Oh no, dear lady. Here you have all the blessings of a lovely land. And your lovely hedges.'

'Hard to prune, I'm afraid.'

'And yet so beautiful, I could weep. Here. Look. There is a tear.'

Miss Swallow looked alarmed. She wondered if the wine had gone to his head.

'Did you have a difficult journey, Mr Cadmus?'

'I beg your pardon, madam?'

'From that place you mentioned. The island.'

'No, I came here by way of London, where I have good friends. Travel is nothing to me. I take it in my stride.'

That was a mark in his favour. Miss Swallow admired enterprising men. 'And why did you choose us?'

'Little Camborne? I came upon it in a map. Just the tiniest dot in a map of the county of Devonshire. My father had maps of all the counties of England. He was an Anglo-style. Is that the word? And I said to myself, this will be my home. I will call myself a Little Cambornean.'

She laughed. 'What an extraordinary man you are. I don't know what to make of you.'

'Make nothing of me, dear lady. Take me as I am. I am your devoted servant.' At that he rose to leave. 'But we will have all the time in the world to exchange reminiscences. I hope this will be the first of many happy occasions.' He seemed pleased to change the subject. 'And my other charming neighbour?'

'Miss Finch.'

'Finch and Sparrow. A nest of singing birds! We will make delightful music together.'

'Swallow.'

'I beg your pardon?' He looked quickly at his glass.

'I am Miss Swallow, not Sparrow. Not that Sparrow isn't a lovely name. It just doesn't happen to be mine. May I?' She took up the bottle.

'Oh no. I must pay my respects to our dear neighbour before it grows too late.' He gave a last admiring look at the room, taking in the ormolu clock, the figurines of shepherds and shepherdesses, the china cats, the miniature portraits, the framed photographs, the painted boxes, the small jugs and vases, and all the other mementoes of an uneventful life. 'You have a delicate taste, madam. I salute you.'

After she had closed the front door she returned, flushed and excited, to her armchair where she went through the conversation word for word.

A short while after Mr Cadmus came up to the cottage of Miss Finch. She was at the door almost as soon as he had raised the knocker, but she waited for several seconds before opening it. She did not wish to be seen to have hurried. She had of course observed him entering the cottage of her neighbour, and had timed the length of his visit to Miss Swallow. She was naturally irritated that he had chosen to visit her friend first, but she was determined not to let her annoyance show. 'Who is it?'

'Your new neighbour, my dear lady. Mr Cadmus.'

She opened the door with a flourish. 'Delighted. Come in, Mr—'

'Cadmus.'

'What an unusual name.' She led him into her sitting room overlooking the front garden. It was not filled with clutter or with bric-a-brac, as he had expected, and instead gave the impression of simplicity or even severity. The walls were painted white, and a portrait of a young woman hung in a frame of green and gold. A sideboard of highly polished oak was matched by a circular table of the same material upon which stood a tall and stately vase of the deepest scarlet.

'This is most enchanting,' he said. 'I see you are a woman of discernment.'

'Well, I have been complimented before.'

'Of course you have. I hope you will find these to your taste.' He presented her with a box of chocolates subtly different from the one he had given to Miss Swallow; it was slimmer and longer.

'And I *do* have a sweet tooth.'

'I had hoped so.'

'Sit where you like, Mr Cadmus.' The chairs were in a modern style but, as he discovered, surprisingly comfortable. 'I think mulled wine is best at this time of year. I make my own.' She returned with two large silver goblets. 'Now I need to know all about you. I don't stand on ceremony. Where are you from?'

'I come from an island, dear lady, in the Mediterranean—'

'That is very interesting. What island precisely?'

'The name would mean nothing to you.'

'Let me be the judge of that.'

'Caldera.' He said the word very quickly.

'I don't know it.'

'We are small. We are under two hundred persons.'

'Rather like Little Camborne.'

'Oh no, dear lady. Here you have all the blessings of lovely land. And your glorious gardens.'

'Hard to keep up, I'm afraid.'

'And yet so beautiful. I could weep.'

After he had gone she wondered whether she should telephone Miss Swallow. No, she could wait. She wanted to savour the exhilaration of this short meeting. For a while she sat with her head back, staring at the ceiling. *I never asked him his first name*, she realised.

Chapter 2

Montmorency

Millicent Swallow hated the Hammersmith house ever since she could remember. She was now thirteen, but her anger and resentment had grown. It was of dark grey stone with a decoration of red brick of no discernible pattern. She hated the fact that when relatives came to stay she was sometimes obliged to share a bed with her mother or even, worst hell of all, with her grandmother. She watched them when they washed their breasts in the kitchen sink, to save the hot water of a bath, and stared at her grandmother when she climbed upstairs with a chamber pot. She hated the smells of the two women when they took off their corsets. When they called out to her in the morning, 'Millikin!', she blenched. There was no way out of this. She was trapped in the little house, with all its smells and its dustiness.

She kept a budgerigar, Clementine, in a small cage in her bedroom. One afternoon her grandmother opened the the door to the cage, in order to clean it, and Clementine flew out. Pursued by the old woman the bird fluttered, and faltered, but eventually escaped out of the open bedroom window.

Millicent had never forgiven the woman, and indulged in a hatred that was almost joyful in its intensity. She believed that her grandmother, out of malice towards her, had deliberately released the bird. But she took care not to show her anger. She remained outwardly polite and amiable. Her mother and grand-mother had endless arguments and rows that led to screaming matches. In one of them an incautious reference gave her the impression that her real father had left home just after she was born. She was soon convinced that the two women had driven him away, so that now she was trapped with them. Her grand-mother would hurl plates or saucers at her mother, whereupon her mother would walk out, shutting the door very loudly as the grandmother called after her 'And what about the poor child?' Millicent was always shaken by these episodes, which only increased her resentment and distaste for both women.

At the bottom of the little garden was a wooden shed that contained a miniature toy dog, gardening tools, a rusting lawn-mower and several half-empty tins of paint. It was here that Millicent would come when she wished to avoid the others in the house. She felt that she had concealed herself, and could spend long periods in solitary meditation. She had not yet outgrown the shaggy toy dog. He was still her friend and adviser. He sat astride one of the tins of paint, his four legs akimbo. His name was Montmorency.

'They have become wild beasts again,' she told him. 'Screaming and carrying on. As if the neighbours can't hear. Of course they can. I know Mrs Wilson pities me. But I don't want pity. I want them to be arrested.'

'And what would happen then?' Montmorency asked her.

'They would be sent to prison. That's what I would like.'

'You are talking about your ma and grandma.'

'Call them mother and grandmother.' She was silent for a moment. 'What am I supposed to do?'

'There is nothing you can do.'

'But why should I be trapped? I have nothing to say to them. I want nothing to do with them.'

'They are your family.'

'I *hate* families. I hate mealtimes. I hate listening to the wireless. I hate *them*.'

'But what would you do without them?'

'I would survive. I'll be old enough next year to leave school.'

'And then what would you do?'

'I don't know. Become a nurse. Or a typist. Something like that.'

'Or a nun?'

'Why are you staring at me?'

'I'm not staring, Millicent.'

'Your eyes look like fire.'

'It is the light of the sun setting. It shines through the window at this time of day.'

A curious auditory illusion of this area was the apparent sound of waves breaking against the shore, accompanied by the crash of crumbling cliffs. Everyone recognised the noise and justifiably explained it as the roadworks for the new motorway. But Millicent knew better. She believed it to be another beach and shoreline just beneath the surface of the earth. They would find the stairway when they were older.

Millicent often held such conversations with Montmorency in the privacy of the garden shed. Unfortunately they were both quarrelsome by nature, and there were occasions when she would snatch up the dog and hurl it to the other side of the hut before breaking down in tearful apologies. Sometimes she would sing to him, cradling him in her arms. Sometimes she would lay him down to sleep, a small cloth over him as a blanket.

There was a call from the house. 'Milly!' It was her grand-mother. 'Supper's ready. It's your favourite!'

'What is your favourite?' Montmorency asked her.

'Anything they don't have to touch.'

She had two more terms at school, and was intent on making her plans for the future with Montmorency. They whispered together.

Weeks passed and Millicent's frustration grew. On Thursday nights her grandmother would prepare a batch of chips in a frying pan greased with fat. The fat would then be allowed to cool overnight to make dripping. Millicent knew well enough when her mother and grandmother had fallen asleep; she was familiar with the rhythm of their breathing and snoring that could be heard through the paper-thin walls of the little house. She waited until she could wait no longer. Two months later, silently she opened the window of her bedroom and climbed down the stairs; she crossed the living room into the kitchen where the pan of fat lay beside the oven. She turned on one of the gas rings and lit it with a long match. As the fat seethed and bubbled she opened the door into the garden. She went back to the stove, and then threw another lit match into the pan. The fat burst into flames at once, and at that moment Millicent ran out into the garden and closed the door behind her. As soon as the flames took hold of the house, she began to call out 'Fire! Fire!' She knew that her mother and grandmother slept well, and kept her voice low. But the smoke was now creeping about her and she screamed in earnest. Some windows were opened. 'Fire! Fire!' In the confusion the fire brigade was called by a young neighbour, Peggy, from a telephone box at the corner of the street.

By the time the firemen came, it was too late to save the lives of the two women trapped in the flames. It seemed to be little short of a miracle that the girl had survived and was quite unhurt. Of course she broke down in tears when told about her mother and grandmother, and she was for a while inconsolable. She spent the rest of the night sitting in the kitchen of a neighbour, drinking tea. She was questioned gently by a police detective on the following morning. Yes, she had smelled the smoke and heard the sound of fire; instinctively she had opened the window of her little bedroom and, driven by fear, she had jumped down to the garden. It was a distance of only a few feet, and she had not been injured. Still, she could not help but limp a little.

When the fire took hold of the house, she never heard any sound from her mother and grandmother; they must have beeen smothered as they slept. She took out a handkerchief and blew her nose.

'You had a lucky escape, young lady,' the policeman said to her.

'Lucky?' She blushed.

Her aunt Helen came to collect her that afternoon; she was now Millicent's most prominent living relative; and she was very tearful. She was wearing a large black hat, and Millicent noticed with disgust that she had a perpetually dripping nose. 'You poor thing,' she said, as she threw her arms about the girl. Millicent was carrying Montmorency, who was only slightly singed. She gently disengaged herself from her aunt's embrace.

Millicent had already decided that she did not want to attend a new school. She would be fourteen the following month, and had no need to do so. 'You know,' she told her aunt after living with her for a month or two, 'I think I might be a good nurse.' Aunt Helen was delighted. It would take this difficult girl off her hands; she had in fact two nieces who had looked on her for support and protection during the war. As well as Millicent Swallow she had a second niece, Maud Finch. There were many such extended families in wartime. But, with the shortages, two were too many.

Aunt Helen was in charge of the local Women's Institute and, according to administrative practice, served on the board of governors of the local sanatorium on Ealing Common.

The sanatorium was under the auspices of the Roman Catholic bishop and, according to the strict regulations, even the youngest nurses were addressed as 'sister'. They dressed as plainly as nuns in a convent, and tried to be equally demure. Millicent was recruited without discussion. Nurses were needed. As a very junior nurse – now known as Sister Swallow – she was assigned a cubicle with another young trainee, Sister Appiah, who had a habit of tearing photographs out of the *Barbados Gleaner* and pasting them into a large red volume. Her principal interest was in the many beauty contests on the island and it was rumoured that Sister Appiah had taken first prize in one of them; so she was known by the patients as Sister Beauty, when in fact Millicent believed that she was on the plain side. Millicent had in fact taken an immediate dislike to her, and waited for a chance to cause her trouble.

In the winter of 1944 an epidemic of dysentery spread across West London that particularly affected the frail with vomiting, diarrhoea and abdominal cramps. There was such an overflow of fluids, of all varieties, that the nurses were happy to delegate their work to the trainees. All of whom, including Sister Appiah and Sister Swallow, were called to duty as a result. Millicent already regretted having joined the profession. One evening Millicent knocked quietly on her aunt's office door in the sanatorium, at the end of a long corridor. 'I think,' she said, 'that you ought to come with me.' Her seriousness and quietness affected her aunt, and slowly they tip-toed along the corridor.

They walked through the three wards, accompanied by such a cacophony of groans and tears that Millicent put her hands up to her ears. 'Don't do that, sister,' Aunt Helen rebuked her. 'It creates a bad impression. We are all God's children.' At the same moment both women heard the distinctive sound of Caribbean music, vey close to the cha-cha-cha, which could only have come from the nurses' day room. Helen stared at Millicent. 'Is this why you called me?'

The girl nodded and then bowed her head as if in shame. She knew very well that the blame would fall on Sister Appiah. 'Say no more about it,' Helen told her. 'There are more ways than one way to skin a cat.'

Within a fortnight Sister Appiah and the other revellers had been transferred to work in a mental institution at Hounslow, and Millicent had the luxury of the shared cubicle to herself. Space was still comparatively cramped, however, and a few days later there was a knock at her door. 'Sister Millicent! Sister Millicent! God be with you!' Immediately she sensed an intrusion. The matron was accompanied by a young woman of indeterminate age who continually brushed her hair across her face with a nervous gesture.

'I am reserving my special ones to your care,' Helen told her. 'This is Sister Finch.'

So what was so special about this pale-faced brat? The fact she was Millicent's cousin was known only to Aunt Helen at the time. Favouritism was not popular in those years of combat. They were soon left alone to compile 'notes' on their sick and grieving patients, many of whom seemed to Maud to be close to death.

'Well, Sister Finch,' Millicent said. 'You have flown to the right nest. Finch and Swallow. Our parents named us after two birds caught in a storm. No, not a storm. A tempest. Thunder and lightning.' She gave an involutary shudder.

After a period of recuperation Maud Finch had been enrolled at the municipal hospital on Ealing Common; both her parents had died in the previous year, during the recent epidemic. Another nurse was a blessing. She now agreed to share her house at Lambeth with Millicent Swallow, who, after the death of her mother and grandmother in the fire, was looking for a new home. She was of course also to be trained at St George's; it was a catchment area for females who could be prepared for war work. As a result, the two young women became natural companions.

Maud had been 'seeing' a young man, Harry, who was employed in a department store off Oxford Street as a draper's assistant. Millicent had been keeping a close eye upon the younger girl's behaviour. On one Saturday evening Maud was setting out for a date with Harry at the Bermondsey Pleasure Garden in the grounds of the old abbey. 'Now,' Millicent told her before he arrived at the door. 'Don't you be allowing any "how's your father".'

'Why ever should he do that?'

'He's a man, isn't he? Men have sweaty hands. You just feel them, and you'll see.' Millicent did not trust Harry; she disliked his camel-hair coat and his brilliantined hair. Still, Maud was now sixteen and could make her own life.

It was sixpence each to enter the pleasure garden, and Harry paid. He also bought a pitcher of beer from a stall in a circus tent, and pointed out the barrage balloon floating overhead, which filled her with a vague dread. Maud was not accustomed to drink. 'That's my girl,' he said, as she attempted her first glass. 'Get that down you, girl. There's more where that came from.' She now realised that he must have been drinking earlier in the day; his speech was slightly slurred and he exaggerated the wrong words. 'Feel like a walk among the trees? Of course you do. Nothing wrong with trees, is there?' He went back to the tent and bought another pitcher of strong ale. 'This'll do you good, Maudie girl. Get a bit of colour in your cheeks. Hold on a mo. I'm just going to pop behind this bush.'

He unbuttoned his trousers and, to her astonishment, began to urinate. She had never seen anything like it before, and quickly began to walk towards the public spaces of the pleasure garden. He caught up with her and put his arm around her shoulders. 'It's a usual thing, isn't it? You see dogs doing it. You see dogs doing all sorts of things. Isn't that right? It's a dog's life, Maudie.'

He was walking her towards the canopy of trees, but she did not struggle or call out for fear of making a scene. 'Here we are. This is lovely, this is. Nice and comfy. You just lie down, my princess. Harry boy will look after you. I can promise you that.'

He lay down beside her, watching her out of the corner of his eye. 'You and I can have a little game. Fancy that, do you? No harm in it, is there?' He touched her leg, and she pulled it away with a gasp. 'Did that frighten you? It wasn't meant to.' He then took hold of her leg and pulled it back towards him, at the same time putting his hand up her skirt. 'Here we go round the mulberry bush,' he said. He unbuttoned his trousers and lay on top of her. 'Nice and pink, princess. Nice and pink.' He took down her knickers. 'Here we go, here we go, here we go. Up the Gunners!' He entered her so forcibly that it would have seemed, if anyone were watching, that he was in fact stabbing her. When he rolled off her, he stared up at the sky. 'You won't be saying anything about this, princess, will you? You being a nurse and everything.'

Maud had to conceal her shock and hysteria from Millicent; no one could know. She told her that she had developed a migraine, possibly from excessive study, and took to her bed in a darkened room. She would not eat but would sometimes wander around the house with an expression that seemed to Millicent to be one of dismay or despair; Millicent knew very little about migraine, and concluded that these were some of the symptoms.

Maud then began to suffer from abdominal pains, but refused to visit the local doctor. 'You're looking very peaky,' Millicent told her. 'You should take some iron pills.' When Maud missed her period, she still refused to consider the possibility that she was pregnant. She told herself that it was simply the result of stress. Yet within a fortnight she knew; her knowledge came not from any outward signs, but from an inner sense that could not be contradicted. She was carrying a child.

For some months she was able to disguise her condition and attend the municipal hospital. She wore large knitted sweaters and dresses that concealed her shape. She believed that there was no reason why she should not be able to hide her pregnancy until she reached full term. No one would ever know of her humiliation. Yet there soon came a time when it was too late for prevarication or concealment with her cousin. The signs were too urgent and too insistent. She walked calmly into Millicent's room.

'I'm having a baby.'

'A what?'

'A *baby*. A human being.' Then she sat down and told her the story of the rape in the Bermondsey Pleasure Garden.

Millicent was the first to bring up the subject of abortion. In her work she had heard of certain powders, and of certain instruments.

'I don't want it to die inside me. I don't want to carry a corpse around night and day. What if it began to rot in my belly?'

'But it doesn't happen that way.'

'How do you know? What if it begins to stink?'

'You're upsetting yourself, Maud.'

'No. I want to see it come out of me naturally. Then I will decide what to do with it.'

In due course there began the first contractions. Millicent had already taken a course of rudimentary hospital procedure, and immediately boiled a kettle of water. She washed her friend and then prepared for the delivery. 'Don't push too hard,' she said. 'It will come naturally. Yes, I see its head. It will just drop out.'

Maud found herself staring intently at the wallpaper. It seemed to be moving of its own accord.

The baby eventually emerged and seemed to be searching blindly for its mother's breast. It was crying, but Maud sensed an apology in its wail. Millicent had been considering the unexpected birth with Montmorency, and both had agreed that the baby must die. After fifteen minutes the placenta had emerged, and Millicent now cut the umbilical cord with a vegetable knife. The two girls looked at one another for several seconds. Then Maud nodded. Millicent took one of the two pillows on the bed and thrust it down over the baby's small body. It did not cry out, and only seemed restless under the unexpected weight until it was finally still. 'Now,' she said, 'you must get rid of it.'

'How?' She looked around the room, as if seeking a hiding place.

'Your handbag.'

'My handbag?'

'A shopping bag. Anything.'

'Then what?'

'You dump it. Take it to the river. It will be washed down to the sea. Or the estuary.' She really had no idea what she was saying. 'It doesn't matter. It won't have anything more to do with you.'

'But what if it floats to the surface?'

'It won't. In any case it will be dark. Go to the bridge after midnight.'

'I will be seen on the bridge.'

'Not if you're quick. Don't lean over the side to watch it fall. Keep on walking.'

Wearing a dark coat, and holding a black handbag, Maud walked the quarter of a mile to Lambeth Bridge. It was a little after midnight, and the street was empty; but she was startled by any sound. She continually suppressed the urge to scream. When she heard footsteps she froze; but the steps passed down a side-street, and the silence returned to the bridge. She walked more quickly, and soon came up to the embankment wall.

She was tempted to throw the bag over the wall, getting rid of it at once, but then she realised that it might land on the foreshore. So she steeled herself to walk onto the bridge. As soon as she knew she was above deep water she flung the bag into the river; she did not hear it drop. She had already walked away. It was done. A car's headlights dazzled her as she crossed from the bridge into the road. She stood, startled and unable to move, as the driver sounded his horn and swerved away from her.

He stopped the car and got out. 'Are you all right?'

'All right?'

There was a police telephone box by the side of the bridge;

he walked over to it and picked up the receiver. Within a few minutes a police car had come up to them. The driver was still trying to calm her when the policeman noticed the large patch of blood on her skirt.

'Perhaps,' he said, 'you were looking for something.'

'Yes. That's it. I was looking for something.'

'What were you missing?'

'I think it was a child.'

'A child? Your child?'

'That doesn't matter now. He's safe.'

'But you know what happened to him.'

'I don't know. I don't know where he is.'

'So why are you here?'

'Why am I here? I can hear the river flowing down to the sea. It takes everything with it.'

'I think, miss, that you should come along with me. You'll catch your death out here. We need to find you somewhere warm and comfortable.'

He placed her gently inside the police car but, as they began to drive towards the station, she became more agitated. She wanted to know where they were going. When they reached the entrance to the station, she would not go in. 'There is a river there. I can't go through it. There are things in it I don't want to see.' She was given a chair in a corner of the police reception where she sat very still. She kept her eyes fixed on the floor until a doctor arrived to examine her. It soon became clear that she had recently given birth, and the presumption was that she had consigned the baby to the river. At the end of the war the number of abandoned babies had multiplied, and the Thames was one of the largest repositories for the unwanted and the illegitimate. The policeman already had suspicions.

'German?' he asked her.

She did not know what he meant. 'POW?' he added. 'They're the ones.'

Maud was taken to her own hospital on Ealing Common, where the matron on duty was called to supervise her. It was, to her dismay, Aunt Helen. Helen had seen so many cases of infanticide in these months that she prescribed some barbiturates before putting her in the care of Millicent. She had already suspected that there was some collusion between the two women over the premature birth and murder of the baby, but she preferred to stay silent. 'I can imagine,' she told Maud, 'but I do not have to be told. War is bloody enough.'

'Our room is nice and comfy,' Sister Swallow said as they walked down the corridor after this unexpected meeting. 'I'll get you cleaned up. At this time of night the shower will be free. Those policemen didn't take very good care of you, did they? But at least they didn't charge you with anything.'

The ward was well ventilated for the benefit of the patients. Sudden breezes or gusts of wind lifted up the white plastic partitions from each bed, and on these occasions it seemed to Maud that the soul of the patient was unusually disturbed. But she became accustomed to the atmosphere of the sanatorium.

She was sure that no one could find out about her previous life. Fearing a scandal but fearing exposure all the more, she wrote a letter to the teachers' training college explaining that she had decided to emigrate to New Zealand, where young teachers were in short supply. So the story of Maud's past was completely concealed.

After a few months Maud had sufficiently recovered to take part in the simple education of some of the other inmates. She had suddenly announced to a junior doctor that she believed she had once been a teacher. A teacher of English, she thought. Or perhaps of history. Still, she was happy to coach the patients, especially those who were illiterate. Within a few months Maud and Millicent had settled down together in St George's Hospital, just as they had in the house in Lambeth, and seemed quite happy with their joint life. They were, it was said, like sisters.

Chapter 3

Tesco

Miss Swallow just happened to be walking out of her cottage when Mr Cadmus appeared in his front garden. 'What a lovely morning,' she said. 'Bright and clear.'

'You have made it brighter, Miss Swallow.'

'Now that will never do, Mr Cadmus.'

'Theodore. I am named after an emperor of Byzantium.'

'Theodore.'

'Imperial coinage.'

'I will remember it.'

'You rise early in the morning, dear lady.'

'I was just about to call on Maud. Miss Finch.'

'Oh yes?'

'We share a taxi on Fridays into Barnstaple. Shopping day.'

'Taxi! But you must let me drive you both!'

'Oh no! We couldn't hear of it.'

'You will be doing me a great favour, dear Miss Swallow. You will be showing me your countryside.'

'But the petrol—'

'A mere nothing. I, too, must shop. Am I not flesh and blood?'

'I will want to have a word with Maud. Miss Finch.'

'Please.'

Miss Swallow walked the short distance to her neighbour's front door. Maud Finch could tell from her ring that something was afoot. From her upstairs window she had seen the two of them talking, and she came quickly down the stairs.

'Maud, Mr Cadmus has kindly offered to drive us into Barnstaple.'

'*Drive* us?'

'Yes, dear, in his car.' They looked at each other with barely suppressed excitement.

'Can we do that, Millicent?'

'I don't see why not.'

'He hardly knows us. We are still practically strangers.'

'We are no longer young nurses. It may shock you, Maud, but we are past the age of forty.'

'It has crossed my mind.'

'It may have occurred to you, then, that we are adults. He is not abducting us, Maud, he is driving us to Barnstaple.' She raised her head slightly. 'I think it would be rude to refuse. Besides, we will be his guides. He wants to see the countryside. Now wrap up. It is rather brisk.'

Theodore Cadmus had parked the car along a narrow track that ran past the side of his cottage. The two ladies waited for him on the grass verge in front of their gardens. 'Where do you want to sit,' Millicent Swallow asked her companion, 'front or back?'

'I really don't mind.'

'I think I should go in the front. I'm better at directions.'

If Maud Finch resented this, she did not show it. She had already become accustomed to it.

Once they were comfortably seated, Millicent took charge. 'We will first of all take you through the village, pointing out the various places of interest as we go.' Maud clutched her handbag as they set off with a sudden spurt.

'Coming up on our left, Mr Cadmus, is the post office and general stores.'

'Very expensive, actually,' Maud murmured.

'Quite so. Yet sometimes a necessary expense. It is run by the Watsons.'

'A very nice couple.'

'Although, Mr Cadmus, you may find them a little common. They come from London. He was a policeman, I believe.'

'I bow to your judgement, dear lady.'

'Down here on the left is the public house. The Nell Gwynne.'

'I have heard of that fascinating lady,' Cadmus murmured.

'Not one of England's finest, I'm afraid.'

'But how pretty she looks on that painted board.'

'Artistic licence.'

'An English pub has for me such romance. I have read of it all my life.'

'We don't go in,' Miss Finch replied.

'Oh no.' Miss Swallow did not want to be left out of the conversation. 'The noise on Saturday nights! Sidney tries his best, but—'

Sidney worked behind the bar of the Nell Gwynne. He had arrived at Little Camborne with a Gladstone bag and a marine compass. He had told everyone that he was a diver by profession, but this had made very little impression.

'If you turn left here, Mr Cadmus, this little road will take us to our church.'

'Ah! A thing of beauty.'

'We *are* proud of it.'

'It goes back to the seventh century,' Millicent Swallow added. 'Although most of it is later. Our vicar is very keen on history.'

'A learned priest. My ideal.'

'He is not exactly a priest,' Maud Finch told him. 'That is something you probably won't understand. He is a vicar.'

'But he is a man of God?'

'Oh yes,' Miss Swallow replied. 'His sermons are lovely.'

They now made their way to Barnstaple, past muddy fields and farmyards, past old stone walls and patches of surviving forest. Millicent Swallow considered that Mr Cadmus was driving too fast, and occasionally looked back at Maud to signal her concern. Miss Finch professed to ignore this and instead addressed him on the subject of Devon in general and Barnstaple in particular. 'We *are* lucky here, Mr Cadmus, with the weather and the views. It's a terribly *sleepy* county, but we don't mind that. Haven't you noticed? That the air makes one rather drowsy?'

'I am never tired, Miss Finch. I am always ready. Always prepared.'

'That is very sensible of you. There is the river Taw. Very serene, as you can see. I think you will like Barnstaple. It has a certain dignity, if you know what I mean.'

'I do indeed. Dignity is very delightful.'

'And we must visit the pannier market,' Millicent Swallow said.

At that moment the car swerved violently and almost came off the road. Mr Cadmus had been forced to avoid a fox that had ran out of an adjacent field. A moment of silence followed, broken by a little cry or mew of distress from Miss Finch. Millicent turned around. 'Are you hurt, Maud?'

'I don't think so. I don't know.'

'You look perfectly all right to me.'

'It was the shock of it.'

'My apologies, dear ladies. It would have been unwise to hit the fox. And I think we are intact, are we not?'

'If you could go a *little* slower,' Millicent asked him.

'Of course. We will be the proverbial snails.'

'And then,' Maud said, 'we could all do with a nice cup of tea.'

When they arrived at Barnstaple Miss Finch got out of the car very carefully, as if she were afraid of breaking into pieces after her ordeal. 'I feel a little dizzy,' she told her friend.

'Tea,' said Millicent firmly.

On their visits to Barnstaple the two ladies always frequented the Old Tea Room by the castle mound. It was managed by Jennifer Pound, one of the inhabitants of Little Camborne. She was astonished that morning when they brought in with them a strange-looking gentleman wearing a cravat and a bright yellow overcoat. 'This is our new neighbour, Jenny,' Millicent told her in a tone of barely concealed excitement.

'Is that right?' She had a marked accent. 'Good day to you, new neighbour.'

'And a very good day to you, my dear. My little circle of acquaintance is growing all the time.'

'You speak good English.'

'My mother. She came from Bridport. That is why I love Devon so much.'

'I thought you said that she came from Exeter,' Maud said.

'To me, dear lady, all is new and exciting.'

Miss Finch and Miss Swallow looked at each other. There was still much to learn about their neighbour. 'We will have a pot of tea,' Maud Finch said. 'Unless you—' She turned to him.

'A tiny espresso, if you please. Very dark. Very sweet. It stimulates me.' Miss Swallow put a hand up to her throat.

'They haven't found him yet.' Jennifer Pound had returned to their table with their cups and saucers.

'Who is that, dear?' Maud Finch was only mildly interested.

'The rapist. They're calling him the beast of Barnstaple.'

'A *rapist*. Oh my goodness.' Miss Swallow had not caught up with the local news.

'It happened four nights ago. Outside the cinema.'

'Oh my *goodness*.'

'And then two nights ago. By the leisure centre.'

'This is terrible,' Millicent Swallow said. 'No one is safe these days.'

'It could be anyone.' Jennifer Pound enjoyed bad news. 'It makes you think. It might be someone who comes in here, for all I know. Appearances are deceptive.'

'I am told,' Maud Finch remarked, 'that the most dangerous criminals are often the most harmless-looking men.'

'All too true, dear lady,' Mr Cadmus interjected. 'I myself have known the most damnable villains with the look of choir boys. All Europe is full of them. Adventurers. Charlatans.'

'I don't doubt it. One does hear . . .' Miss Finch's opinions of Europe were not to be expressed to a foreigner.

'I won't be able to sleep tonight. I know it.' Miss Swallow was alarmed. 'To think of this person only a few miles away.'

'You should be fine.' Jennifer Pound was smiling at her. 'He only attacks young women.'

'So *far*. You don't know what he might be *capable* of.'

'You will just have to look under the bed.' Jennifer Pound was still smiling.

Maud sipped her tea delicately. 'Before you work yourself up into a panic, Millicent, I suggest we visit Tesco.'

Mr Cadmus wanted to accompany them both in the supermarket, but the ladies insisted on separating from him. They did not wish to reveal their purchases to a relative stranger. In fact they bought only the familiar merchandise of any household, but Mr Cadmus was more adventurous. He purchased smoked duck, pickled herring, a tin of sauerkraut and a large box of pretzels. When Miss Swallow saw him unload the goods in front of the girl on the till, she raised her eyebrows in surprise. Miss Finch was too flustered to notice.

'Did you remember detergent?' she asked her on the journey home.

'Yes.'

'And the Flash?'

'Oh yes. But I am torn between the solution and the cream.'

'I prefer the solution. It has a lovely fragrance.'

It seemed to Miss Finch that Mr Cadmus was a little subdued; he was humming a tune she did not recognise, and he was driving more steadily than before.

'And how did you find Barnstaple?' she asked him.

'It is admirable in itself. It lacks romance, perhaps.'

'Not very warm praise.'

'I cannot flatter, dear Miss Finch. I can only speak the truth as I see it. I know that honesty is not always the wisest policy, but I cannot help myself. That is Cadmus.' His eyes moistened as he turned momentarily towards her. 'Forgive me.'

'Oh, there is nothing to forgive. I agree with you entirely. Barnstaple is *not* romantic. It has other qualities, perhaps, but romance is not one of them.'

'It is charming in its own way.'

'Of course.'

'But, you know, charm is only skin-deep.'

'I agree.'

Miss Swallow had woken from a slight doze a few moments before. 'Did you say that Barnstaple lacked character?'

'Not at all. It does have character.'

'Surely *that* is romantic.'

'Ah, Miss Swallow, romance is an elusive thing. It is airy.

It is like a perfume or a breeze. Have you not felt it in the past? Have you not sensed it?'

'I really could not say, Mr Cadmus.'

'You are among friends. But there will come a day when you confide in me. I know it.'

Chapter 4

Poor Isolde

The parrot had been restored from quarantine. Mr Cadmus had come out of his car with the cage in his hand, now complete with its illustrious occupant. The ladies came to their respective windows, and lightly applauded the arrival of the bird, noticing particularly the deep amethyst patch of colour above its beak.

'You must be properly introduced to Isolde,' he told them on separate occasions the following day. 'We must make it a formal ceremony. We must sing.'

This did not seem a particularly good idea to the ladies, but they concurred; they had been eager to take their first look into his cottage. At the appropriate hour, six o'clock on Tuesday evening, they arrived together at his door. He greeted them both with a kiss on the cheek, a ritual they had now come to expect but not necessarily to welcome. As they entered the cottage Miss Finch sensed a slight but singular perfume in the air that she associated with Chinese restaurants of the better sort.

Miss Swallow was much struck by the flock wallpaper

in the hall. 'Oh, this is lovely. That rose and cream looks good enough to *eat*. Is it damask?' He led them into the room overlooking the front garden and the road. A large rug, with vivid images of elephants and towers, covered the polished wooden floor; a sofa had been placed beneath the window, and beside it a small table with a lamp of green jade. 'I have been to your antiquity shops,' he said. 'I choose wisely.' His expression took in a lacquered writing table, a folding table of ivory, two armchairs of Georgian date, and several upright chairs with embroidered seats. The two ladies were settled on the sofa as Isolde, shifting from claw to claw, observed them with what Miss Finch believed to be a hostile eye.

'What a heavenly room,' Miss Swallow said. 'Very daring.'

'I hope it is not too daring. Too un-English.'

'Not at all. It has a lovely *feel* to it.'

Miss Finch had been staring nervously at the parrot. 'So this is Isolde.'

'Yes. Poor tragic Isolde.'

'Why is that?'

'Can you not tell? She lost her mate. Tristram. They were inseparable. Like one bird. Yet the day came when he was felled.'

'His heart?'

'Diarrhoea.'

Isolde was largely blue, with specks and streaks of green, together with an amethyst patch above her curved beak.

'How did she cope?' Miss Swallow was immediately sympathetic.

'Cope? She was inconsolable. But she bore up.' The bird, still glaring at Miss Finch, took up a peanut and cracked the shell with its beak; Miss Finch considered its tongue, fleshy and bulbous, to be faintly obscene.

'I have been told,' Miss Swallow was saying, 'that parrots can last a lifetime. Is it true that they can live for sixty years?'

'Fuck off, you silly bitch.'

The three of them looked at the cage with amazement and some alarm. The bird had spoken.

Mr Cadmus was indignant. 'She has not learned that language from me.'

'From the quarantine,' Miss Finch said. 'You never know what types might work there.'

'Piss off, you old cunt.'

Miss Swallow put her fingers to her ears, as Mr Cadmus hastily threw a black cloth over the cage. The parrot squawked, and then fell silent.

'The bird is not to blame,' Miss Swallow said. Miss Finch was not so sure.

'Some ghastly person has taught her those words. Wait till she catches sight of Montmorency. That will scare the feathers off her!' She laughed, but stopped abruptly in the fraught cicrcumstances of Mr Cadmus's household.

Cadmus was distraught. 'I can't think what is coming over her. Never before has she used such language. And to guests!'

'Be patient with her,' Miss Finch told him. 'Teach her beautiful words. Such as puppy or candy floss.'

'They would not be beautiful to a parrot, Maud.'

'No, Millicent, but slowly they will replace those horrible expressions. You must exercise her.'

'Exercise a parrot?'

'What do I mean?' She shook her head, frustrated. 'Exorcise. Do we have a little crucifix to hang among her toys? And perhaps a bird prayer?'

Millicent was not impressed by Maud's suggestion. 'What do you want, Maud? A black mass? You should complain to the government, Mr Cadmus. These quarantine officials should be sacked.'

Later that evening, after she had retired to bed, Maud Finch heard a loud cackle of laughter from the cottage next door. She could not tell whether it came from the parrot or from its owner.

On Sunday morning Mr Cadmus accompanied the ladies to church. 'I have a liking for English churches,' he had told them several days before. 'They are so simple.'

'Oh, you must come to St Leonard's.' Miss Swallow was enthusiastic. 'You will meet our minister. Tony is such an asset to Little Camborne.'

So on the appointed morning they walked to the local church at the bottom of the little road. A number of villagers lingered by the porch, greeting new arrivals. Mr Cadmus surveyed them with an expression of genuine interest. If I am to flourish here, he might be presumed for thinking, then I must first understand *them*. He was introduced to Ron and Phil Appleby, brothers and farmers, both of ruddy complexion and cheerful countenance. 'Jolly good show,' he said.

'Mr Cadmus is our new neighbour,' Miss Finch told them. 'He comes from the Mediterranean.'

'Oh really? My wife and I are off to Malaga in March.'

'You will find the cathedral enchanting, sir. Not in this style, of course.' He looked up at the façade of St Leonard's. 'Yet absurdly beautiful.' The two farmers looked at him with curiosity; they were not used to finding things absurdly beautiful, or even beautiful at all. They made their way into the church through the medieval porch into an interior suffused with the scent of beeswax, old stone and a curious fugitive perfume. The stained windows had long since been replaced by transparent glass, and a plain wooden table now stood before the old altar. 'I miss my saints,' Mr Cadmus said as they took their place among the rows of wooden benches. 'And where is the Mother of God? She is loveliness personified. She should be here.'

'I thought,' Miss Finch replied, 'that you liked our English simplicity.'

'But it may go too far. What is wrong with a little candle and a pinch of incense? Or a rosary?'

'Idolatry.'

'Then I am a heretic. God help me. Mea culpa, as we say on Caldera.'

When the congregation was assembled the reverend stood before them in his black cassock and white square-necked surplice.

'Grace, mercy and peace from God our Father, and the Lord Jesus Christ be with you.' The reverend's voice was mild and melodic.

'And also with you.'

'This is the day that the Lord has made.'

'Let us rejoice and be glad in it.'

Mr Cadmus did not reply with the congregation. He did not know the words, although he made a mental note to learn them. He would then feel more at home. Miss Swallow offered him her prayer book. He noticed some pressed rose leaves among its pages, and he held one up between his thumb and forefinger as if to examine its intricate structure of connection. Miss Swallow blushed.

The reverend, Anthony 'call me Tony' Beaumont, had the face of a haunted altar boy; he might once have looked angelic, but unknown anxieties had changed his expression. He could not hold a direct gaze for more than two or three seconds; he had a slight tic, at times of stress or perplexity, in his right cheek; he perspired easily, even in cold weather. Yet his voice was as modest and mellifluous as ever.

After the readings of the psalms and the passages from scripture were completed, Tony stepped forward. He began with a homily on the seven knightly virtues, and their relevance to a modern code of chivalry that must include courage, generosity, mercy, justice, nobility, faith and hope.

'Embrace our neighbours,' Tony told them, 'with love and sympathy. The greatest Christian virtues can be exercised in the smallest possible places. Our little village is an example.' Millicent Swallow was suffused with pride, and glanced at Mr Cadmus.

'And if our neighbours do sometimes disappoint us, or behave in unacceptable ways, do not harden your hearts against them. Be patient. Look for the best, and not for the worst. And then you will feel the peace of Our Lord Jesus Christ.'

Miss Finch watched as Mr Cadmus wiped the side of his eye. *He is not a heretic,* she said to herself. *He is a Christian.*

To that Christian's astonishment, two or three guitars were brought out from the vestry and given to members of the congregation, who began to strum their instruments or clap their hands in what seemed to be the beginning of some kind of pop anthem. Absentmindedly Tony began to stroke the long hair of a chorister, and the boy smiled.

'Oh Jesus, Jesus,

Oh Jesus, Jesus, set me free

Oh Jesus, Jesus, shine on me

Send your vibes

To the tribes

Of Israel, oh Jesus, Jesus.'

Mr Cadmus had never heard anything like it, and he looked in surprise at his two companions. Miss Finch remained silent, her lips pursed, but Miss Swallow made a series of half-hearted attempts to join the singing. She seemed to have some difficulty with 'vibes', before which she hesitated.

The singing came to an end after two or three repetitions of the chorus. The echo of the guitars lasting only a moment against the old stone walls of the church, which seemed to defy music. A silence ensued in which Tony prepared himself for the recitation of public prayers, and then he turned around to face the congregation for the final blessing.

'The Lord bless us and preserve us from all evil, and keep us in eternal life.'

'Amen.'

'Let us bless the Lord.'

'Thanks be to God.'

Tony walked slowly from the church and stepped onto the gravel path, beyond the porch, to greet his parishioners. He was introduced to Mr Cadmus, who bowed low and seemed about to kiss his hand; Tony quickly brought out his handkerchief in order to blow his nose. 'God bless you, Father, for your truly moving words.'

Tony Beaumont was not used to being addressed as 'Father', and seemed at a loss how to reply.

'It is his first time,' Miss Finch said apologetically.

'Not in church, surely?'

'In one of *our* churches.'

'Si quis autem in verbo non offenderit, hic perfectus est vir.' Mr Cadmus held out his hands.

'I didn't quite get that,' Tony said, clearly confused.

'I don't think it matters,' Miss Finch told him. 'If it was in Latin, it must have been good news.'

Miss Swallow also reassured him. 'He looks so happy. He has that lovely smile.'

★

'I hope,' Mr Cadmus said as they walked back to the Coppice, 'that I made a good impression on your priest.'

'The *vicar* was very pleased to meet you,' Miss Swallow replied. 'He particularly asked that you be invited to our do next week.'

'Your *do*?'

'Yes, we're having a winter fair for the church restoration fund. We all bring wintry things and sell them.'

'What is a wintry thing?'

'Anything, really. Scarves. Gloves. Christmas puddings. Mince pies. Overcoats.'

'I shall be bringing mulled wine,' Miss Finch said.

'Oh, your very splendid mulled wine! But what can a mere foreigner give?'

'That woollen hat,' Miss Finch replied. 'The one I saw you wearing yesterday morning.'

'But it is so old.'

'No matter. It looks very handsome, if I may say so. Russian, I think.'

'Sicilian.'

'Even better. It is the first Sicilian hat I ever saw.'

So a week later, on Sunday afternoon, the hat was taken in great state to the winter fair held inside St Leonard's. Stalls had been set up on each side of the central aisle and, as he visited each one in turn, Mr Cadmus introduced himself. Most of the villagers in fact already knew his name or recognised him as 'the foreign gentleman at number two'. He beamed at jars of pears in brandy, at children's mittens, at scented candles, at balaclava helmets, at candied orange and all the other paraphernalia of an English winter. Sidney had decorated the windows and window sills with pine cones painted red, blue and white.

'My mulled wine is going *very* well,' Miss Finch told

Cadmus. 'It might almost be foreign.' Meanwhile Miss Swallow was 'helping out' with the raffle which, at five pounds a ticket, was considered to be a little expensive even for a good cause. The prize was a bottle of vintage brandy, donated by the landlord of the Nell Gwynn.

The electric lights of the church were switched on in the late afternoon, just as the shadows began to lengthen, and the raffle tickets were tipped into a large wicker-work hamper. Tony Beaumont stepped forward, riffled through them, and then picked out number twenty-eight as the winner. 'I do believe,' Mr Cadmus said to no one in particular. 'Yes. Twenty-eight! I have it!' To general applause he accepted the bottle and waved it above his head.

A few minutes later he watched with interest as Tony Beaumont poured all the notes and coins into a black attaché case that he snapped shut. As he did do he looked up at Mr Cadmus, and managed only an uncertain smile.

'Dear priest, you must pray for your safety along these country by-ways.'

'No, no, Mr Cadmus. We are a happy congregation.'

'And honest, too?'

'To be happy is to be honest.'

'You must preach that to my little islanders on Caldera. It may come as a surprise to them.'

'Your island is not familiar to me. But I have heard the name. Could it be connected to Saint Paul?'

Theo shook his head. 'Alas not.'

'I cannot quite recall the context. But I am sure there is one. Everything connects, does it not?'

Chapter 5

Hairy Men

'Have you heard? There's been a robbery at the post office! An *armed* robbery. All the police are there!' Miss Finch had run quickly up to Miss Swallow's door.

'Is anybody hurt?' Miss Swallow asked her.

'I tripped on my herbaceous border. And now my keys are all mixed up. Hurt? I don't think so. But there was an ambulance there! And someone said a gun!'

'Oh my God!'

Mr Cadmus came to his door. 'What is the excitement?'

'A robbery!' The ladies almost said it in unison.

He stepped out. 'Where?'

'The post office.' They might as well have said the Wild West, for all the hysteria.

If anything, he was more curious than his neighbours. 'Well, I suggest that we walk to the high street. And keep our eyes open.'

The whole village seemed to come out of doors, spilling into the road beside the post office. Voices were raised with accounts of the event, from a pistol being fired to shrieks heard in the neighbourhood of the girls' school. Neither occurrence could be verified by the policeman. No one was sure what, if anything, had been taken. A photograph of the queen had been turned upside down, and some cigarettes had gone. That was all. How was Mrs Watson? She had been helped into the ambulance, white and shaken, but she seemed to be unhurt and complained about water on the knee. Excitement mounted again as Mr Watson came out of the post office, accompanied by another young policeman in civilian clothes; the postmaster was greeted with scattered applause, which he received with some dignity.

Someone remarked that it might have been the work of the beast of Barnstaple; the rumour spread immediately and within minutes, if not sooner, it was clear that the robbery had been the work of the rapist. He had been in hiding, like an outlaw, and now needed money. Millicent Swallow was already in a state of some alarm. The beast had come to Little Camborne! Who knows? He might even have crept past the Coppice. She would not be able to sleep tonight.

Mr Cadmus had observed the young policeman with interest and now went up to him. 'You can follow his foot-prints in the frost?'

'Of course.'

'I suspect that he would have made for the nearest stream and followed its course. I would search for the first wood you see going north towards Barnstaple. Look out for cheap cigar-ettes.'

Maureen Simpson approached Maud Finch. Mrs Simpson, recently widowed, was the personage through whom and from whom most of the village gossip flowed. She lived along the high street, and her net curtains were constantly in move-ment. 'This is a terrible thing, Miss Finch.'

'Perfectly ghastly.'

'I'm sure I saw somebody in the high street early this morning.'

'Oh really?'

'Just before dawn. It was ever so dark. But I can't sleep.'

'Your old trouble?'

'The cold nights bring it on. Anyway, there was someone there. Of course it might have been your new neighbour. The foreign gentleman.'

'Oh?'

'He sometimes gets up very early in the morning and walks through the village.'

'Does he?'

'Sometimes at night, too. I dare say he has something on his mind. He is always *peering*.'

'I dare say he is—'

Her reflection was interrupted by the arrival of Alfred Crozier, the owner of the village garage that also did service as a gardening centre. 'These people should be shot. What colour was he?'

'We have not yet been told,' Miss Finch told him. 'No doubt it will all come out in due time.'

'He could have been a gypsy. He won't be from around here.'

'I didn't know we had any gypsies.'

'Haven't you heard? They've got onto the common at Marbury. What do they call themselves? Travellers. They'd better not travel around here. They're nothing but trouble.'

The little group was now joined by the 'handyman' of the village, John Abbot, known always and only as 'Jack'. He was carpenter, plumber, gardener and builder all at once. Miss Finch had only recently asked him to repair the fence of her front garden. 'Did you hear the shot, Jack?' He lived immediately opposite the post office.

'Oh yes. I called the police. I would have got the bugger – pardon my French, Miss Finch – but he ran out the back way. I never saw him. I heard Mrs Watson wailing, though, poor soul. So I rang for an ambulance.'

The thought of anyone wailing unnerved Miss Finch; it sounded so foreign and, somehow, superstitious. So she was happy to hurry back to the Coppice, where all news could be safely shared. Soon after she returned, Miss Swallow came to her door.

'Nothing was taken, apparently, except for some cigarettes and sheets of postage stamps.'

'Stamps are very expensive these days, Millicent.'

'True. But are they the sort of thing to satisfy a robber?'

'Why did he fire his gun? If he did have a gun at all.'

'They all carry guns. Apparently he was caught off guard when Mr Watson came downstairs in his pyjamas,' Maud added.

'The brute.'

'It is too horrible to contemplate. Imagine the beast of Barnstaple having been in Little Camborne.'

'It is most unlikely to be the same man, Maud.'

'Whyever not?' Miss Finch almost sounded aggrieved.

'It is not the same kind of crime. Rape and robbery do not mix.'

'But he might be capable of *anything*.'

'It will not be the same man. Trust me.'

Miss Finch was a little relieved, but still restless. 'I wonder if Theodore is back yet. I saw him talking to that policeman.'

'Who?'

'Theodore. Mr Cadmus.'

'I wonder at your using his Christian name so soon, Maud.'

'But he is a friend now, Millicent. Did you not choose that Swedish hat for the raffle?'

'You will be calling him Theo next.'

'Oh, that would be going too far. And I cannot trust myself to set foot in his house while that – that *thing* – is there.' She was referring to Isolde.

'He lets it out of its cage, you know. I can hear it flapping about.'

'*Don't.*'

Mr Cadmus himself could now be seen approaching the Coppice, and Maud went to the door. 'Theodore, we were just talking about you.'

'Sweet things, I hope?'

She led him into the front room where Miss Swallow was waiting impatiently for his arrival. 'Have you heard any more?'

'The police have already begun to search the neighbourhood. They fear that he might have concealed a motor-bike.'

'Then he will get away.' Miss Finch was very sure.

'Oh dear,' said Millicent Swallow.

'Your countryside is very big,' he said. 'Enormous.'

'I have always hated motor-bikes.' Millicent was now alarmed again. 'Horrible big things. Somehow I always think of them as *hairy*.'

'The men are hairy, dear. Not the bikes.'

'I have tried to explain to you, Maud, that this man is highly unlikely to be the rapist.'

'That's easy for you to say.'

'I agree with the gracious Miss Swallow. A rapist is not likely to turn into a robber. That would be too much of a pantomime.' The two ladies stared at him. 'Yes. I know about your English theatre. It is very diverting. Heroes and villains and such like.'

'The difference is, Mr Cadmus . . .' Maud Finch had reverted to a more formal address. 'The difference is that in *pantomime* we know who the villains and the heroes are. We have no such luck in Little Camborne.'

'But you have luck in other things, dear lady. Such luck with the pretty fields and streams.' Mr Cadmus clapped his hands together, as if to terminate the interval. 'I know. We will go for a walk to banish bad thoughts. It will be the thing to do.'

So, on this chilly December morning, they wrapped up well. One route across the fields was familiar to the two ladies. Just behind their road was a hill that led directly to a wood of tall pines, and so they walked among trees and clumps of bush to the summit. 'At times like this,' Maud Finch said, 'I wish I had a dog. Just a little one.' As the track came to the edge of the wood, it turned left towards a stile that led into a neighbouring field. The two ladies were quite used to surmounting it, but Mr Cadmus insisted that he 'lend a hand'; this was a cause of momentary embarrassment, as he grasped each of them firmly and eased them across with a 'Hola!'

They were still on the eminence of the hill, and from here they could see one of the tributaries of the Taw moving quickly between the meadows. 'This is what I am here for,' he declared. 'An enchantment.'

'But surely your island was charming,' Millicent Swallow asked him. 'I don't recall its name, but—'

'The name is not important. It has its charms, yes, but it was cruel. Hard rock. Beating sun and no shade between the dust and the bright blue sea. Only olive trees and goats.'

'But that sounds delightful. Quite like Monte Cristo.'

'I beg your pardon, Miss Swallow?'

'It's nothing. Out of an adventure.'

'It is about a man,' Miss Finch told him, 'who wants to get revenge on all of his enemies.'

'Is that so? He would be very ingenious, then?'

'I can't really remember the story now.'

'Neither can I,' Miss Swallow added. 'But it made such an impression on me at the time.'

'On my little island, we had many adventures. Smugglers. Pirates. And so forth. It was hard rock only suitable for hard people.'

'But you are not hard, Theodore.' Miss Swallow was almost affectionate.

'No? Perhaps I am the exception.' They had come into another field, slowly making their way down the slope, when he stopped. 'Hello. What is this?' It was a thermos flask together with a torn t-shirt and an empty tobacco tin. 'Perhaps our robber did not have a motor-bike, after all.'

Miss Finch and Miss Swallow looked at each other in alarm. 'You don't mean to say,' Maud Finch asked, 'that he has been here?'

'Someone has, dear lady.'

'Surely it must be a tramp?' Millicent Swallow was becoming agitated.

'Yes. This is a possibility. Let us walk on.'

'Do you really think that is wise?' Maud Finch was also becoming nervous.

'What we must do,' Miss Swallow said, 'is to go back quickly to the Coppice and telephone the police.'

'I agree with Millicent. Remember, Mr Cadmus, that he may still have his gun.'

'You must speak to them. I am a mere foreigner, after all.'

'But I saw you speaking to that policeman.'

'A moment of madness. He never asked me for my name.'

They walked back quickly. Miss Swallow seemed to be alarmed by every rustle in the undergrowth around them, and sometimes looked back to make sure that they were not being followed. 'Look. Over there,' she said suddenly. 'There's someone running through the field. The other side of the stream.' They stopped and peered in that direction, but they saw nothing. 'There *was* someone,' she said. But there was nothing in sight, only the motion of the wind that gusted through the hollow coppices in a strange simulacrum of the human voice.

From her cottage Miss Finch called the police station, and went over the incidents of the eventful day one more time with the added excitement of the tobacco tin and the torn t-shirt.

Chapter 6

Dum Di Dum Di Dum

The three of them had agreed to share a Christmas lunch. Mr Cadmus had joined them for the service at St Leonard's, where among the parishioners assembled in the pews there was general satisfaction at the arrest of a young man on suspicion of the robbery at the post office. He came from the neighbouring village of Lower Tawbridge, once more arousing an ancient discord between the two communities. In the remote past they had two distinct meeting places, that of the Camborneans at the Scole Stone and that of the Tawbridgites at Crab Oak. The opponents now played an annual football match on a field located on the boundary between them.

'What's a young lad doing with a gun in the first place?' Jack Abbot was asking no one in particular.

Mr and Mrs Watson, now recovered of their former good humour, were still at the centre of attention, and it was expected that Tony would say a few words about their ordeal when he addressed the congregation.

Tony was in fact at that moment confiding in Miss Finch.

'I have found a really admirable stained glass woman in Bideford. What would you say to "Christ in Majesty"?'

'Isn't that a little high?'

'Not at all. Very English.'

Miss Finch herself was the object of general village approval. Her telephone call to the police, after the discovery in the field, had assisted in the arrest of the young man from Lower Tawbridge.

After the service was over they 'slipped back', as Miss Swallow put it, to the Coppice for Christmas lunch. It had been agreed that the two ladies would prepare the food, while Mr Cadmus would provide the drink. Miss Finch had made the pumpkin soup and the Christmas pudding, while Miss Swallow had cooked the turkey and the rest of the traditional lunch. By common consent they had agreed to use Miss Swallow's cottage as their dining room; it was less forbidding than that of Miss Finch, and did not contain the cantankerous Isolde.

All went well. Mr Cadmus had chosen two bottles of delicious Sauvignon for the soup and, for the turkey, several bottles of Merlot had been purchased at Oddbins in Barnstaple. The ladies were not accustomed to drinking at lunchtime but he insisted on filling and refilling their glasses at every opportunity; they did not resist, however, on the shared understanding that this was a very special occasion.

'When I was at the ladies' academy in Caxton,' Miss Finch said, 'some of the girls stayed with us over Christmas. Ex-pats and so forth.'

'You were a teacher?' Mr Cadmus asked her.

'Of mathematics. And sometimes of astronomy. The school had its own telescope.'

'I knew it! I knew you were a woman of learning!'

'You must tell Mr Cadmus how I placed you there,' Millicent said. 'It was touch and go.'

These were the memories Maud hated. Millicent herself had a tendency to exaggerate and over-dramatise the incidents of her life, to the extent that she entangled herself with preposterous stories.

'No doubt it was.' Miss Finch did not care to prolong the conversation. 'It was so long ago now. I was at Caxton for fifteen years.' She sighed. 'They will all have forgotten me by now.'

'Nonsense, Maud. You were the star teacher.'

Those had been the days when Maud sought refuge with the help of Millicent, in the hope of forgetting her recent past. With the memory of the dead baby, she still could not cross the Thames.

'But your knowledge will have sown a million seeds, dear Miss Finch.'

'I don't think algebraic fractions feed many minds, Mr Cadmus.'

'No. Your passion for learning. Your delicacy of feeling. If only I could have heard your lessons on the Milky Way!'

Miss Finch was touched, and allowed her glass to be filled once more. 'I suppose I unveiled some mysteries.'

'Ah, sweet mystery of life.' Miss Swallow was already in reminiscent mood. 'Nelson Eddy sang it.'

'And you, Miss Swallow, you also have seen something of life.'

'I cannot deny it, Theodore. I have had my fair share of feeling.'

'A toast,' he said, 'let us have a toast to feeling.'

They raised their glasses. 'It is better,' Miss Swallow said, 'to have loved and lost than never to have loved at all.'

'You have said a beautiful thing, Miss Swallow. It brings tears.' Indeed, at that moment she brushed her eyes with her handkerchief.

'I think,' Miss Finch said, 'it is from Tennyson. Or someone similar.'

'May I say what I believe? I believe that both of you ladies came to Little Camborne with wounded hearts. Am I correct?'

Miss Swallow blushed and reached once more for her handkerchief, but Miss Finch, having no particular desire to reminisce, resisted his blandishments.

'I came here, Mr Cadmus, because the properties in Little Camborne were left to me by my aunt.' But then she picked up her glass, and relented. 'Old ladies are supposed to have their secrets.'

'Old? Never old. You have a youthful mind. You are like the Christmas holly. Evergreen. And you, Miss Swallow – Millicent – I see in your eyes that you are a young woman still.'

'That's not what I see. Every time I look into a mirror I wonder how I grew so old so quickly.'

'Do not say that, Miss Swallow.'

'But I must say that. When I think of all the time I've wasted, doing nothing really, I could weep.' Maud Finch noted that her friend had drank freely and was more animated than usual. 'I have never really *done* anything at all.'

'You do not *do,* dear lady. You *are.*'

'I am afraid that is a little too deep for me. What am I?'

'You are a magnificent creation!'

'Oh dear.'

Maud Finch gazed at him, wide-eyed. This was perhaps going a little too far, even for Christmas Day.

'Both of you are the most splendid ladies I have ever known.' He held out his arms. 'You are enchantment.' As he spread out his hands he knocked over the glass of Merlot from which he had been drinking, and some of the wine spilled from the table onto the beige carpet beneath.

'Salt!' Maud Finch cried out. 'Put salt on it!'

Millicent Swallow rushed into the kitchen and came back with a packet of Saxo that she sprinkled liberally over the wine stains. 'I think,' she said, 'that this excitement calls for another drink.'

They were all now in a thoroughly good mood. 'You must have had admirers, Maud.' Mr Cadmus raised his glass to her.

'I dare say I did, you naughty man. But you must not press me too far.'

'You still get a Christmas card from that old flame,' Miss Swallow said. 'I can't remember his name.'

'Do you mean Frank?'

'The teacher.'

'The *headmaster*, Millicent. He was a very distinguished man.'

'So what became of him?' Mr Cadmus was very sharp.

'The drink,' she said. 'He was a victim to gin.'

'I have seen your *Gin Lane* by the renowned Hogarth.'

'Nothing so sordid. Just a gentle decline.'

'You told me that he used to wet himself.'

'Millicent!' She put her fingers up to her ears. 'Spare Mr Cadmus the details.'

He laughed. 'Not at all. I am becoming interested in poor Mr Frank. When did you see him last?'

'And to think,' she said, brightly changing the subject, 'that in five days' time it will be 1982.'

'I'm looking forward to 1984.' Miss Swallow had begun to perspire.

'I don't think it will be like the book, dear.'

'No?'

'I presume it will be like any other year.'

'That would be terribly disappointing.'

'But my dear Maude, who knows what any year will bring?'

Mr Cadmus was becoming more confiding. 'An adventure? A journey? A romance?'

'Nothing,' Millicent Swallow said, 'ever seems to happen to me.'

'Then you must prepare yourself to be changed. Wish for a strange event. Then it will occur.'

Miss Swallow got up very suddenly. 'Oh dear. We have forgotten the Christmas pudding.'

The pudding had been placed on the kitchen table, and was now quite cold. 'No matter,' he said. 'I will set it on fire.' He poured a large quantity of brandy over it, and then lit it with a match. Miss Swallow screamed as a blue flame leaped upwards and seemed almost to touch the ceiling. Mr Cadmus laughed and clapped his hands. 'Now we will be wild. We must have music! Music! Where are your records, Millicent?'

Maud Finch, also now curiously animated, knew where her neighbour's collection was to be found. She took out an LP of Frank Sinatra's *Songs for Swingin' Lovers!* and, to the sounds of 'Anything Goes', Mr Cadmus began to waltz Miss Swallow around the room. He may have led her too quickly since, after a minute or so, she staggered and fell back into an armchair with an expression of surprise and delight. Mr Cadmus was still upright. 'Miss Finch,' he said, 'may I have the honour?'

'Wait a moment, Theodore.' She went over to the gramophone, and moved the needle to the beginning of 'I've Got You Under My Skin'. 'This is my favourite.' They began a dignified and even solemn minuet, not inappropriate to the music, but it was interrupted when Miss Finch succumbed to a violent attack of hiccups. 'I am so sorry,' she said, between spasms.

'Drink out of a cup backwards,' Millicent suggested, 'or hold your breath.'

'No, no. I have the perfect cure for dear Miss Finch. Allow me.' He put out both of his hands, and tweaked the lobes of her ears between his thumb and forefinger. 'That is the Mediterranean way.' Miss Finch gave one immense sneeze, and the hiccups then subsided. 'This makes the trick, you see.'

'Does the trick,' she replied. 'Grazie mille.'

'Oh, my dear lady, you speak Italian!'

'Oh no. I went to Rome many years ago.'

'There is always something new and enchanting to learn about you.'

'When I was a mere girl,' Miss Swallow said, 'I went to Madrid. It was very hot.' She was staring into space.

'You are both women of the world.'

'That sounds naughty.' Miss Swallow pretended to be shocked.

'If only it were true,' added Miss Finch. 'Get me another drink will you, Theo?'

'By all means. And you, Millicent?'

'Oh no. Really, I couldn't.'

'Not in this season of great joy?'

'It would be rude not to, Millicent.'

'Well. If you put it like that—'

So both ladies were given large glasses of brandy. The pudding had been forgotten. Two hours later Millicent Swallow was sick into the hedge which separated her property from that of Cadmus, while Maud Finch leaned against the wall and gazed into the night sky ablaze with stars. 'Look how the floor of heaven is thick inlaid,' she began. 'Dum di dum di dum.'

Chapter 7

The Earthquake

One evening in early spring Maud Finch observed a stranger going up the path to Theodore Cadmus's front door; he was wearing a trilby and long white raincoat, and carried a leopard-skin suitcase. 'Now this is *very* foreign,' she said to herself. 'I wonder what he is doing here?'

The man put down his suitcase and stared at the door for a few seconds before ringing its bell. When Cadmus opened the door Maud Finch heard an exclamation in Italian that might have been one of anger or astonishment.

'Che cosa fai qui?'

The stranger's reply was soft and melodious. It sounded like an entreaty. There followed a short silence before the stranger was allowed to enter. Quickly she went over to the wall that divided her cottage from that of Theodore Cadmus, and put her ear to it. At the same moment, on the other side, Millicent Swallow had executed the same manoeuvre.

They heard the low rumble of Theodore Cadmus's voice interrupted by the higher tones of his visitor. Neither of the women could of course follow the argument, even if they could have heard the voices clearly, but it was certainly an animated one. *Really*, Millicent thought to herself, *it is very like an Italian opera.* There was suddenly a loud exclamation and a crash; a table had perhaps been knocked over or a vase flung to the ground. Maud Finch stepped back from the wall in alarm, and Millicent Swallow put her hand up to her mouth in shock.

There followed a long silence, in the course of which the two ladies resumed their postures against their walls. Maud was so excited that she had quite forgotten her newly prepared cup of tea, now grown cold on the kitchen table; Millicent had developed cramp in her left leg, but was prepared to endure the agony in order to maintain her position.

Much to their surprise they now heard laughter; the Italian stranger then began to croon in a fine tenor voice what sounded like a love-song. Once more silence followed, broken only on occasion by a murmur of conversation. The two ladies, a little weary after their vigils, both, separately, prepared themselves for an evening's television, a hot drink and bed. Maud Finch believed that she had heard gasping noises in the night, coming from Theodore's bedroom adjacent to her own, but she dismissed the idea as fanciful.

The following morning Cadmus came out into his garden, still sadly denuded after the previous owner's depredations. Almost at once Maud Finch put on her shapeless gardening hat, in colour and appearance like a large toadstool, before filling a plastic watering can at the kitchen sink.

'Your snowdrops have gone, Theodore, I'm afraid,' she said as she stepped out into the garden.

'They melt with the sun.'

'No. The flowers. Like drops of milk.'

'Oh. The pretty white things? They have already left me?'

'Never mind. There will be others waiting to come out.

In this climate, they hibernate. They lie hidden and then burst out.'

'That is good to know.'

'Here are my crocus. And my narcissus. And do you see? Millicent already has a mass of daffodils.'

'Your English daffodils are famous.'

'And just think of them buried out of sight only a few weeks ago.'

'Very remarkable.'

She sensed a sudden movement, and looked up at Cadmus's house. At that moment Millicent came out into her garden. 'Good morning, gardeners,' she said to them. 'I seem to remember that Mr Herrick had a lovely splash of bluebells. Over there.'

'Another surprise,' he said.

'Oh. And an amethyst plant.'

'What is amethyst?'

'It looks like a flower, but it is not a flower.'

'They are associated with witches,' Maud said. 'They summon demons. Some of them are poisonous.'

'Is that so?'

'Heart failure.'

'I must be careful not to collect any.'

'You never know what is lurking in an English garden.' Millicent was almost coy.

'Ah. Then it is like the Garden of Eden. There may be a snake. Is that so?' Cadmus pretended to search the ground.

Neither woman dared to broach the question of Cadmus's unexpected visitor – it would seem like prying – but they occasionally directed glances at the silent cottage.

'And what,' Maud asked him brightly, 'are your plans for today?'

'I intend to be quiet. I will listen to some music. To my beloved Brahms.'

'Oh, do keep your windows open. I can listen to him while I'm weeding.'

There was no Brahms that day, however, and the windows remained closed.

On the following morning Maud Finch observed Theodore Cadmus walking down the path towards his car parked outside the garden gate; she also noticed that someone else was sitting in the car. It was the stranger, wearing the white raincoat. She opened her front door and walked rapidly into the garden. 'A lovely morning for a drive, Theodore.'

'Yes indeed.' She peered into the car, and the stranger gave her a weak wave.

'An old business partner,' Theodore said rapidly, noting the gesture. 'He speaks no English.'

'Is he from your little island?'

'He is from Venice.'

'Venice? I have always wanted to go there!'

'It is not all it seems, dear lady. Many ghosts.'

'Ghosts don't frighten me, actually.'

'These ghosts would frighten anyone. Goodbye for now. I am driving my friend into Barnstaple.'

'Oh, I may see you there. I'm popping in to see my hair-dresser. Maurice on the high street.'

'Is that so?'

'Perhaps I will see you there.'

'Oh no. We are only going to the bank.' He spoke very quickly.

'Banco! Banco!' The stranger turned around and gave a 'thumbs up' sign to Maud.

'Arrivederci,' she said. She stood watching as the yellow car proceeded down the road but then, thinking that this might be bad manners, she stepped back and went into her cottage. Millicent was almost at once on the phone.

'Where were they going?'

'Barnstaple. The bank.'

'The bank?'

'Banco. His friend seemed very nice.'

'Did you speak to him?'

'We exchanged a few words.' They paused for thought. 'I have to go into town,' Maud added. 'It's my hair day.'

'I might come with you.'

'Might? Or will?'

'Well, all right. I will join you.'

They called their regular taxi driver, who lived in the next village. He had been expecting them, since they always travelled to Barnstaple on the same days of the month.

When they arrived in town, and stepped onto the high street, they looked about brightly in the hope of seeing Cadmus and his foreign friend. They walked past the National Westminster bank very slowly, and almost collided with the reverend Tony who was hastening down its steps. 'Good morning, ladies,' he said very briskly, 'well met by moonlight. Or something like that. Toodle pip.' Then he was on his way.

'He seemed a little flustered,' Millicent said.

'He is a vicar.'

'I didn't know vicars used banks.'

'Oh, don't be so ridiculous. They earn a salary, don't they?'

'I suppose so. But God and Mammon – there they are!'

Cadmus and the Italian were walking along the opposite side of the high street, apparently deep in conversation. Cadmus was carrying a briefcase in his left hand, while the Italian was talking rapidly between bouts of high nervous laughter.

'Do we go up to them?' Millicent asked.

'Oh no, I don't think so. They may be discussing business.'

They both heard at the same moment a small rumble, like the sound of distant thunder; silence fell for a few seconds, and suddenly the ground beneath their feet began to tremble. It shook so much that the two ladies had to steady themselves against the railings of the umbrella shop. Someone screamed, but then all was quiet once more. They looked at each other wide-eyed.

People began running out of the shops along the high street, and almost collided with each other in their eagerness to find out what had happened. Strangers began to talk excitedly together, while friends and neighbours indulged in mutual astonishment. Maud and Millicent looked across the street, but Cadmus and his companion were not to be seen. Sidney was standing there, waving his arms wildly.

When the two ladies entered the Old Tea Room they were met by a high level of chatter; the small earthquake had of course brought the customers together. 'I am told,' Jennifer Pound was saying, 'that there is a fault line between here and Bideford. In dry weather you can see it.'

'Do you think it could open up?' someone asked.

'I am told,' she replied, 'that there are caverns beneath Rowley's farm.'

'That's where he keeps his money.'

'That's where he keeps his wives.' This remark was followed by general laughter, in which Maud and Millicent did not join. The drama of the tremor having passed, their thoughts had returned to the Italian stranger.

'I am glad,' Millicent said, 'that his old friends come to see him.'

Maud was gazing at the castle mound. 'Only one old friend. And I'm not even sure that he is a friend.'

'They seem to know each other very well.'

'That doesn't necessarily make them friends.'

'You are very suspicious. Just because they're Italians, I suppose.'

'That has nothing to do with it. Why did they go to the bank?'

'Perhaps his friend needed to cash some traveller's cheques.'

'Maybe. But I think something odd is going on.'

'What a mind you have.'

'At least I've got one.'

'Maud! That was unnecessary.'

'Was it?' She soothed her right temple with her fingers. 'Apologies. That earthquake has unsettled me.'

Jennifer served them tea.

'I wonder who else might be visiting him.'

'You take too much interest in Theodore, Maud.'

'That's rich. Coming from you.'

'Whatever do you mean by that?'

'You are not exactly disinterested.'

'He is my neighbour.'

'Perhaps you would like to be something more.'

'What?!'

'The way you look at him.'

'I look. And what about you? Lingering in the back garden for a brief encounter.'

'I wasn't the one who presented him with bedding plants.'

'There was an empty patch!'

'I think,' Maud said, 'that this has gone far enough. I suggest that we call a taxi and go home without saying anything further.'

Yet they continued their conversation as they sat in the back seat of the taxi. 'I don't have a *special* interest in him,' Millicent said in a low voice. 'If that is what you mean.' She was silent for a moment. 'And I am sure that he has none in me.'

'I hope you are saying that with sincerity.'

'Why the interest, Maud?'

'I don't want to see you being hurt.'

'How could I possibly be hurt?'

'We are at a sensitive age.'

'Sensitive to what?'

'Oh, you know.'

'Let me say for the last time that I have no romantic interest in Theo. Theodore.'

'I wasn't supposing that exactly.'

'What were you supposing?'

When they arrived back at the cottages, no yellow car and no Cadmus were to be seen. Millicent retired to her kitchen, where she took up Timothy into her lap and began to fondle him. Maud went into the garden and began her much delayed task of weeding. About an hour later Cadmus returned; alerted by the sound of the car the two women hurried into their respective living rooms and watched from a discreet distance. Cadmus came out unaccompanied; he had lost the faintly petulant and irritated expression he had assumed in the company of his friend, and now once more he seemed jovial and energetic.

'Has your friend gone?' Millicent asked him the following morning when they met by chance in the village general stores.

'Oh yes. I took him to the railway station. On his way back to Italy. Terrible weather.'

'Was there not talk of floods?' Maud asked him.

'There is always talk. Never read the newspapers, Maud. They are good only for crossword puzzles.'

Chapter 8

The Rose Tree

The people of Little Camborne were gathering outside the church of St Leonard's on the following Sunday, eager to be given Tony's interpretation of the earthquake. There were still some, among the older residents, who half-believed in divine displeasure and wanted the vicar's reassurance on that point.

They waited on the gravel path, quietly gossiping in the sunshine. The earthquake had brought on Mrs Harris's baby, which had just slipped out without any fuss. Three goats from Mr Honey's farm had disappeared; they had either fled in fear or they had been swallowed up. The cracks in the earth had sealed themselves, as was customary in the region, and there was no sign of disturbance. This was one of the geological curiosities of the district. 'The land hereabouts has always been known for its slips and falls,' Ron Appleby muttered, looking to his brother for confirmation of the terrain. 'What about that silver amulet?'

Phil Appleby scowled. Found treasure was not a subject for public discussion.

'All sorts,' Jack Abbot added. 'I can remember when we

found a small bag of amethyst stones. We put it on the altar and prayed for Saint Paul to bless it.'

'There's too much sleeping and dreaming in this parish.' Jennifer Pound disapproved of such unhealthy speculation. 'You would think that there was a dobie behind every rock.'

'A dobie?' Mr Cadmus was intrigued.

'A dobie, Mr Cadmus, is a hob. It is not to be believed. It is a bog vapour. Mist. Vapour.'

'But is there not a Hob Lane behind the pannier market?'

'A mere whimsy.'

Little Camborne seemed to Theodore Cadmus to become more and more mysterious. Meanwhile Maureen had embarked on one of her interminable stories. 'I know about hobs,' she said. 'A little while after I got into bed,' she said, 'I heard someone walking up and down the street outside.'

'Was it a man?' Mrs Watson asked her.

'There was nothing to be seen.'

'What would it have with you?' Mrs Watson was laughing.

'You know what it was, Eileen Watson. What about the incense in the front porch? That never left us.'

Half an hour had passed. Tony had not arrived, with his usual beams of welcome, at the door of the church. Could he have been engulfed by the earthquake? The housekeeper was called to the upstairs windows of the vicarage. She disappeared for a few moments, and came back looking confused. 'His bed's not been slept in.'

The announcement caused immense excitement.

Mrs Simpson now recalled seeing Tony boarding the train with suitcases at Barnstaple. He told her that he was delivering old bound bibles to the British Library.

Mr Cadmus, in turn, remembered Tony leaving the bank. 'I think,' he said to Maud in a low voice, 'that the Reverend has purloined our treasures.'

'You're not implying . . .?'

'And why not? It is an affliction of many priests.'

'But surely not in the Church of England!'

'Is it not human? It is not divine.'

The excited parishioners now asked the housemaid for the key to the church door, which, after much fumbling and struggling, was found. Their boots and sensible shoes clattered down the flagstones of the nave as they looked for they knew not what. But what was this? A relic of pre-Reformation days, a golden monstrance buried for three hundred years in the garden before being restored, had gone from its accustomed place by the font. The famous bag of amethyst, supposedly blessed by Saint Paul, had also disappeared from the altar. The collection boxes were empty, and the money put aside for church pamphlets and Christian news had gone; even the piggy-bank for the crisis in West Africa had been rifled.

Could Tony be a thief or an accomplice? 'This is now a crime scene,' Millicent announced. 'We mustn't touch anything.'

'But I've already touched the collection box!' cried Maud.

'You will have to give them your fingerprints.'

'The police were summoned from the station at Bromerscombe. 'This is a first,' the sergeant said as he clambered out of what seemed to be a rather battered police car. 'You might call it divine intervention.'

Maud looked at him with relish. 'That might be considered blasphemous.'

He ignored her. 'So the vicar has gone.'

'With the loot,' she answered.

'We don't call it that any more, Mrs—'

'It can't be swag,' Millicent said. 'That bag of amethysts has gone from the high altar. That is no swag. That is sacrilege.'

'Stolen goods,' the sergeant said. 'Very simple.'

Millicent took great delight in giving a description of the

Reverend Tony. 'Longish hair, which is rather unsuitable for a vicar, and a loud taste in clothes. He always wore brown shoes with black trousers. I should have guessed that something was wrong. On the small side, about five feet and six inches, brown hair with definite streaks of grey, and a curious little stub of a nose. Oh how silly of me. There will be a photograph of him in one of the parish magazines.'

During a thorough search of the vicarage the two policemen found a collection of what one of them called 'unhealthy material'. It was rumoured to include photographs of the reverend in unlikely and obscene positions with other men. This excited the village even more, with reports of homosexual orgies and even black magic whispered in every local shop. Some frightful possibilities, involving Tony, were mentioned. But in the days and weeks that followed, the parish soon adjusted itself. The vicar from the neighbouring market town drove in to give divine service once each Sunday, and the deaconess, June, came in to assist with the congregation. St Leonard's had a long tradition of the deaconess beginning, it was said, when a nunnery lay across the road.

'Have you seen June?' Millicent asked Maud. 'Old Mrs Chuddery is due a visit.'

'She was walking around the cemetery with the warden. He doesn't think there are many spaces left. I'm not surprised. Tony was burying them left, right and centre.'

'You don't think . . .?'

'What?'

'Nothing.' They dropped what might have been a delicate subject, of death by design. Surely not in the Church of England?

The deaconess bustled; June bristled with energy, and was always in motion.

'Excuse me,' she said to a group of parishioners before the first service. 'I was rather hoping that you would bring flowers with you. For the communion table.' She was a tall, thin woman with a natural air of authority that might have seemed to some to be one of condescension. 'Oh, dear Miss Finch, I am sure you have some lovely peonies.'

'I must look.'

'Oh, do! They have such a short season it would be a shame to miss them. Don't you think?'

On first seeing her, Mr Cadmus emitted a soft sibilant sound between his tongue and his teeth. 'Witch! On my island she would burn.'

'Oh, surely not.' Millicent was shocked by this outburst. 'Isn't the punishment too great for the crime?'

'You see how plain she is,' he said. 'Like an ostrich.'

'I think,' Millicent replied, 'that she looks very distinguished.'

'But not necessarily attractive,' added Maud Finch.

Theo glared at the deaconess. 'I can never go into this church again.'

'But what will you do?'

'I will say my private devotions. I have relied upon them before.'

'She is only a deaconess, Theo.'

'It is all the same magic.'

This was an aspect of Cadmus that had not previously been revealed to them. Millicent looked at him with admiration. 'You are very deep, Theodore.'

'I never speak of such things. They are too – too deep – too deep for words.'

'We all have our spiritual side,' Maud said.

'That is so true, Maud. I know yours is very strong. Very rich. As is yours, Millicent. I feel it.' He put his hands to his left breast and looked, as if in appeal, from one to the other. 'This is a special moment for all of us. Wait. I will show you something.' He walked back to his cottage and came out, a minute or so later, holding a flat grey stone. 'The Blessed Virgin stood on this rock.' The ladies looked at one another without expression; they had not been brought up to venerate the Mother of God. 'She appeared in our little town of Foradada forty years ago. High upon a cliff. So beautiful. I, Theodore Cadmus, climbed that cliff when I was a little boy. I brought this down with me. I have kept it ever since. You may touch it.'

Maud stroked it tentatively with her finger. 'What am I supposed to feel?'

'See. Not feel. You have visions, dear ladies?'

'Not as far as I am aware,' Maud said. 'Should we not consult the Vatican?'

'I see a rose tree rising in your garden. One day the rose tree flowers, and a white bird appears. That is a lovely sight, is it not?'

'If it were true.'

'You only believe what you see. Is that so?'

'Something like that. I am a woman, Theodore, I am practical.'

'There can be no doubt about it. It gives me inexpressible pleasure that you are a woman, Maud. I would not have you any other way.'

Millicent was growing restless at the attention lavished on her friend. 'Did you say, Theodore, that you wanted my recipe for carrot cake?'

'Indeed I do.'

'You will have to come in and get it. I can only think it through in the kitchen.'

'And does that mean an adorable cup of tea?'

'If you so wish. I wouldn't want to force it on you.'

'Oh no, I submit. I always submit.'

Millicent, now believing that honours were even, smiled at Maud. 'Would you care to join us for tea?'

'Thank you, no. I have to sew two buttons on my cardigan.'

★

When Maud rose from her bed and walked over to the window, two or three mornings later, she was astonished to see a rose tree growing on a bed of soil close to the cottage; it was of modest size but was already in bloom. 'What on earth?' She said the words aloud. She was for a moment too bewildered to have any response at all; she simply saw a rose tree, pink upon green. But this state of dazed incomprehension was followed by a surge of anger. Theodore Cadmus had planted this tree in the dead of night. There could be no doubt about that. He had entered her garden without her consent. He had uprooted some of her plants, and put this thing in their place. He was a trespasser.

The telephone rang. It was Millicent. 'You must have seen it.'

'Of course I have seen it.' Maud's voice was weak and tremulous.

'Well?'

'Do you think I should cut it down?' She had an image of herself applying an axe to the tree of superstition.

'Whatever for? I think it's sweet.'

'But he came into my garden without my permission. At *night*, Millicent.' She spoke the last words in the manner of a tragic heroine showing exemplary calm.

'He just wanted to surprise you.'

'He succeeded.'

'I think the roses are *lovely*.'

An hour later Maud walked into her garden; she wore a little beret, tipped at a slightly rakish angle, with a brooch fastened to it. She assumed that Theodore was watching her. She went up to the rose tree and gently touched its leaves before picking one of its small flowers, inhaling its scent and then delicately removing and dropping two or three of its petals in a circle. Within a few moments Theodore emerged fom his cottage.

'You see, Maud, a miracle!'

'I think I will be the judge of that.'

'How can you doubt it, Maud?'

'I think the Virgin Mary may have had a little help.'

'You are a very cruel person.'

'Where did you buy it?'

'Money has never changed hands,' he said. 'I tell you, it is a spiritual thing.'

Millicent now came out into her own garden; she had been listening to her two neighbours from a vantage point behind the drawn blinds of her kitchen window. 'A tree is a tree is a tree,' she said.

'That is very profound, Millicent.' Mr Cadmus clapped his hands.

'Wherever did you find it?' She was beginning to resent the fact that Maud had received the gift.

'It was found.'

'You are very provoking, Theodore. I never know what you mean.'

'I am a *tease*, Millicent? Is that what the English say?'

Millicent was surprised. 'I would never call you that.' Maud laughed in what Millicent considered to be a sarcastic manner. She looked disapprovingly at her neighbour. 'Be sure to water it properly, Maud. You don't want it to die.'

'I am sure, dear Milly, death is positively the last thing on its mind.'

Early the following morning Maud looked down on her rose tree, just in time to see a white bird fluttering delicately upon it. The air was clear and bright, and she opened the window to savour the dawn as the white bird seemed to fix its eyes upon her.

Chapter 9

The Christopher

'I know what we will do, ladies. We will make a plan. We will go to London.'

'Oh my goodness.' Maud put her hand up to her cheek.

'I think that's a splendid idea,' Millicent said.

'But it's so far.'

'Nonsense, Maud dear.' Millicent was already very eager. 'We can get the train from Barnstaple. And stay overnight in a cheap hotel.'

'Over*night*?'

'We can take in a show. I would love to see *Cats*.'

'I know a small hotel,' Theodore said. 'Very snug.'

'And cheap?' Millicent was a little brisk.

'They have good rates. It is in Notting Hill, after all. Yet the rooms are very clean.'

Maud was now resigned to the prospect of a London journey that induced in her a sensation of mild anxiety. 'But, Millicent, who will look after Timothy?'

'Gloria will feed it. We will only be away for two days.' Gloria Barlow lived on a small council estate behind the

Coppice, and was sometimes called upon to perform light duties.

'I suppose so.'

'We are only going to London, Maud, not Timbuktu.'

A plan was agreed, and on the next weekend the three neighbours set out on a train to London. As they approached Paddington, Maud became more and more miserable. She did not like London. It was too loud and too crowded, and the grim houses flashing past added to her distaste. Why was everything so dirty?

It did not help that Millicent and Theodore were in high spirits. Ever since they had all boarded the train at Barnstaple they had both seemed to conspire against Maud with delighted speculation about where they would go and what they would see. When they changed trains at Exeter St David's, Millicent decided to buy *The Times* to discover what plays or concerts were being performed that evening. 'Oh, this is too marvellous. Mahler at the Festival Hall. Right by the river.' Maud closed her eyes. '*Or* Brahms at the Wigmore. Isn't it exciting?'

'London is a great whore,' Theodore said. 'It advertises its delights.' Maud did not care for the analogy. 'I am just the pimp. I will take my ladies wherever they wish to go.'

'Good heavens.' Maud stared hard at an inside page of the newspaper. 'A body has been found on the rocks at Ilfracombe. Washed up by the sea. And naked. You remember Ilfracombe, Theo? I think we took you and your friend there.'

'It will be an accident,' he said. 'Or a suicide. Ilfracombe is known for it.'

On their arrival at Paddington, Maud suddenly felt very tired; the whole weight of the city seemed to fall upon her. She was appalled by the noise and confused by the crowds who seemed to swarm around her. 'There are three of us,' Theo said. 'It will be an economy to take a taxi.'

The Hotel Christopher was situated in the neighbourhood of Earl's Court, part of a street of small hotels and rented flats that did not recommend itself to either woman. 'Here we are!' Mr Cadmus said as they took out their suitcases. 'I love the smell of London.' He led them towards the hotel and ushered them into a small hall where a receptionist sat smiling behind a desk.

'Good morning, capitano. Chi non muore si rivede.' The man's black brilliantined hair was tied back in a short pony tail; he was wearing a white short-sleeved shirt, and had a tattoo of a heart on his right arm.

Maud glanced at Theodore. 'Capitano?'

'I was in the army for a while. Nothing special.'

'You never mentioned it.'

'It was nothing special.'

The receptionist had been watching the two women. 'Chi sono quelle due bonazze?'

'He is admiring you, ladies. He is asking me how I have the pleasure of your acquaintance.'

'I am Charles,' the man said. 'Carlo.'

'He is the stepson of my cousin,' Theo added.

'From Caldera?' Maud asked him.

'What a memory you have. No, no. A different place.'

'And how long has he lived in England?'

'You may ask him yourself. He speaks good English.'

'I have been here for eight year.' He had a perceptible Cockney accent. 'Home from 'ome.'

Matilda did not believe that he was wholly respectable. Receptionists should not bear tattoos. 'You do have *three* rooms for us?'

'Three lovely rooms. Kettles and teas provided.'

Millicent and Maud inspected each other's rooms with the unspoken understanding that they would not intrude upon Theodore.

'My room is smaller than yours,' Maud said.

'But you do have a view.'

Maud looked over the street, while Millicent had sight of a side-alley.

'There isn't much in them.' The rooms contained a bed, a chair, a side-table and a wardrobe.

'Cheap and cheerful.'

'Hardly cheap and hardly cheerful, Milly.'

'No, I suppose not.' She sighed. 'Well, we will only use them for sleeping.'

A knock on the door surprised them. 'Are you decent?' It was Theodore.

'Of course we are decent.'

'I hope you like your little nests.'

'They *are* little,' Millicent said.

'But so cosy. So gemütlich.'

'I beg your pardon?'

'It is a German expression. Forgive me.' He went over to the window. 'What a glorious day to see London!'

They came out of the hotel and looked about them. 'Let us go into this interesting avenue,' he said, pointing to Warwick Road, 'and walk up to the Kensington High Street. A short walk will take us to Hyde Park and the famous Round Pond.' So they proceeded on their way.

'Have you noticed,' Millicent said in a low voice to Maud, 'how many foreigners there are? I don't think I have heard a word of English.'

Maud made a circle around her face, with her finger, and mouthed the word 'Arab'.

Theodore was walking ahead of them. He looked over his

shoulder from time to time, and then darted into a newsagent. As soon as he left the shop he looked down the street once more, as if his attention had been diverted. Something fell out of his pocket, and he quickly scooped it up. Maud caught a glimpse of a blue stone.

'If you will excuse me, ladies, I have an errand to perform.'

Millicent looked at him astonishment. 'But we thought you wanted to visit the Round Pond.'

'An appointment I forgot. Very sorry indeed.'

'We will see you in the hotel this evening,' Millicent said very firmly.

'Well,' Maud said as he disappeared down a side-street. 'What extraordinary behaviour. How can he have an appointment? We've only just arrived.' Now that Cadmus had left them, she felt more than ever their isolation in a crowded and noisy city. 'Whatever shall we do?'

'We shall do what we plan to do. We shall go to the Round Pond and feed the ducks.'

'Do you know the way, Milly?'

'Of course. I taught at a primary school in Knightsbridge. In the Fifties.'

'You never mentioned it.'

'I can't mention *everything*.'

They set off down Kensington High Street as if they were going into battle. 'Every colour under the sun,' Millicent said. 'I'm not prejudiced. But why do they *all* have to come here?' Gingerly they made their way along the street, at one point being swept back into a shop entrance by a group of running children. 'I blame the parents, Maud.'

An elderly woman was carrying a can of lager and walking unsteadily towards them. 'She's *drunk*,' Maud said. 'Disgusting. Let's go in here to avoid her.'

They had entered a small shop that seemed to specialise

in alarms, keys and locks where a young man in a dark blue turban looked from one to the other with a friendly smile. 'Are you ladies looking for household protection?'

'Oh no,' Millicent said. 'We live in Devon.'

'But even in the countryside, crimes can happen. Am I right?'

'I am afraid we are very quiet.'

'I think, Millicent, that we have come to the wrong shop.'

As they left Maud glanced at her. 'You have forgotten the beast of Barnstaple. And the post office. In the country there are surprises.'

'I don't like to mention things like that. It lets the side down.'

They crossed the high street into Hyde Park where the sound of laughter, the cries of the children, the insistent gabble of the ducks and geese, all began to weigh on Maud's spirits. 'I don't like these London parks,' she said. 'They are so unnatural.'

'They serve their purpose.'

'What is that supposed to mean?'

'I dare say you would find out if you lived here.'

To this remark, Maud could think of no suitable reply. 'I'm feeling peckish,' she said.

'You've come to the right place.' They walked towards Knightsbridge past the Serpentine.

'I know,' Millicent said. 'Let's go the Spaghetti House. Happy days.' They paused before the large window of the restaurant, its interior still shapeless from the vantage of the sunny street. Millicent put her face against the glass and peered in. 'I wonder if my favourite waiter is still here. Alfredo.'

'They all look very Italian, Millicent.' Millicent quickly drew back from the window. She had seen Theodore sitting at a table with Carlo and another man; he looked angry, and was brandishing a map. Then she sensed a 'click' in her inner ear, as if a table lamp had been turned on.

Chapter 10

The Island

The sailors who painted their ships blue for the sake of camouflage were coming close to the misty island of Caldera. Theodore was lying on the rough bed of grasses on the cliff's edge, watching the changing colours of the sea which reflected the small purple, blue and scarlet flowers scattered all around him. In the cool of the early evening he could savour the scent of the thyme, the heather and the rosemary that lay pressed beneath the weight of his body. From here he could see the grey swifts that nested in the sea caves, swirling in their flight just above the restless sea.

He knew the routine of the ships as well as their crews did. These were the vessels of the islanders who kept a careful watch on the German and English frigates who frequented the contentious area between Sardinia and Italy. They exchanged information and found themselves useful to both sides. The Germans and English thought of them as no better than fishermen, but the Board of the Admiralty in London and the German Admiral Staff in Berlin would have been surprised to learn that the islanders' knowledge of the sea and its tides went back a thousand years.

Theo saw a boat coming around the strip of land that lay to the west. It was an army ship, complete with turret and two guns. 'And who are you?' he said to himself. 'Are you German?' He guessed that the boat had sailed from Sicily and was reconnoitring the waters. A boat from Caldera had already reported its position. He leapt to his feet and followed a stony track that skirted the cliff-top; then he half-ran and half-slid down a slope covered with old olive trees, gnarled and withered.

He was only twelve years old, but he knew every patch of the island. He imagined the world itself to resemble Caldera, a terrain of limestone and ancient rock partly covered in fields of stubble and, in its lower reaches, by plains of rich vegetation. Fruit trees abounded, walnut and hazel, but the gullies were clothed in pine and oak with mossy trunks. Caldera was lined with sea caverns, coves and grottoes, with limestone crags descending precipitously into the sea.

Eventually he crossed the familiar plain of rock, seamed with patches of russet and purple, until he reached the farmhouse. 'Fabio!' He whistled. 'Fabio! A ship!' His older brother came out upon the loggia covered with vines. 'It must be German. Is that not so, Fabio?'

The brothers lived alone in the farmhouse. It was two years since their parents had died of malaria, the evil of an island where in the southern part mosquitoes rose above sluggish streams and swamps. He and Fabio had taken their bodies to Nacoro, the island of the cemetery. A priest lived there with a fisherman who acted as the grave-digger. From the small jetty on Nacoro they dragged their parents' bodies, clothed in shrouds of stitched goatskins, to the white chapel a few hundred yards from the shore. They also brought with them some rings and bracelets of gold that their mother had hoarded for payment. Every family had a small treasury for the funerals. Theo's parents were buried among the hills and fields of stubble to the sound of the cicada and the grasshoppers. The boys took it in turns to row back to their island, satisfying their sudden hunger with coarse bread and the root of the fennel.

The farmhouse never changed. The rectangular loggia, always in the shade, opened into a large room that contained a stove and an old-fashioned olive press. Above the stove was a cuckoo clock and a framed photograph of the pope. A chest of drawers was placed against the opposite wall, on top of which were various small ornaments of pink and green glass. A set of rooms behind the kitchen harboured agricultural implements, piles of lemons and of oranges, and bundles of dried figs. On the second floor, accessible only by a ladder, were the living quarters of Fabio and Theo. They had once been obliged to share a bed but now each brother had his own bedroom; the beds were made of dried goatskin stuffed with feathers, and above them were medallions of the Virgin Mary. The walls and ceilings of the house were blackened with smoke, emanating from the stove, and the only light came from the open door onto the loggia. The hens scratched at the straw that covered the floor.

At the back of the house were two large cisterns to contain the rain that fell from November until April, when the ravines and ridges were striated with white mist and when torrents of water washed away the loose soil by the sides of the streams. Mushrooms sprang out of the damp earth. This was the season when Theo, following the example of his mother, picked the dandelion and the plantain. It was the abundant time. The least scrap of garden was now precious, and he gathered up the piles of dried olive leaves, the remains of dead cacti, cabbage roots and other sweepings and mixed the mould with the rich soil of a plot surrounded by stone walls. Every hollow in the rocky ground of the yard became a natural vessel in which to grow broad beans, or lettuce, or fennel.

From the fields he gathered green almonds, and from the coast he brought back sea urchins with their orange fruit. He did not like the sea. None of the inhabitants of these islands did. He blessed himself before entering the water for fear of sea witches but, in its shallows between the rocks, he could catch with his hands the light brown fish known as cernia. Sometimes he cooked up a thin gruel, known optimistically as zuppa di pesce, but it was at least an addition to their familiar diet.

Once a month they killed a goat, and could survive on its flesh for several days. Fabio, as the older brother, was the custodian of the goats; he was their companion as well as their leader. He knew their impishness, their air of mocking obedience, and their audacity. Yet when he put his knife to the throat of the animal, he had an expression of rapture; any pity had been replaced by a strange and almost impersonal rejoicing.

Every two weeks Theo rowed west to the island of Leucothea, where he bartered goat's milk and vegetables for the local bread. It was the most populous of the islands, some of it so smooth that it looked as if it had been carved by an artist. A cluster of houses, painted white or blue or yellow, lay in the middle regions of the mountain that dominated the smooth plains. Its port was in constant traffic with the mainland, and Theo learned much gossip about the course of the war from the islanders. The English and the Americans had landed in Sicily. The Germans had fought back. The English and Americans were planning an assault upon the mainland. The Germans were about to occupy all of Italy. No one knew what to believe, or what to fear.

On Caldera an image of the saint of the island, Santa Regilia, stood at the end of a mountain path among tall cypress trees; the area, fragrant with the scent of distant blossom, had always been for Theo sacred. There was a spring here, but it was warm and musty to the taste. The boy came from time to time in order to pay his respect to the statue, its colours and even its outline now gone with the wind and the rain; yet for him it retained its power. He always dressed for the occasion. He wore a red handkerchief tied about his neck, and an old Homburg hat that had belonged to his father. He took off the hat now and knelt before the statue. Santa Regilia was the patron of the simple-minded, the innocenti, but of course she spread her benevolence over all aspects of the island.

Theo was asking her to provide a calm sea for his journey to Leucothea, but then on the following day he heard the explosion. In the first moment it sounded like a stone dropped into a pond, but then the blast brought him to his feet. He ran down the path, gulping in breath; he fell badly and gashed his knee but he felt no pain. He could see the smoke rising into the air; he had bitten his tongue and the blood flowed freely into his mouth.

The farmhouse had been struck by a rod of fire, dividing it into two clumps of ruin; as he slowly walked towards it he could see the body sprawled in the yard. He did not want to come too close. Half of the face had been blown away. 'Fabio?' He prodded his brother's left foot with his shoe. Then he kicked it. He screamed out 'Yooooo!' and ran behind the farmhouse to the pen where the goats were kept secluded by silver-green hedges. He unfastened the wicker gate and circled around the animals. But they would not move out of the pen. They looked at him curiously, as if they already knew that Fabio was dead. He ran to the back of the herd and began to chase them through the open gate with screams and curses. When the last of them had fled he lay down and slept.

He woke to the silence and the starlight. When he sat up he could see just ahead, at a depth he could not estimate, a dance of fireflies, silent lights, *fuochi morti*. The odour in the air was that of withered rosemary and cistus, as old as the stars. He shivered and stood up, chastened by his solitude. He could feel grief for his brother's absence, but he did not want to return to the body; he had a vision of the island itself concealing it and laying it to rest. Had it been a grenade, or an aimless shot from a patrol at sea? English or German? It did not matter. But he thought he heard English voices above him, together with the sound of laughter.

He followed a familiar rugged path for some time until he came to a bay beside a beach overgrown with rushes and with sea thistle; above them rose the cliffs, which intensified the darkness all around him. But he knew his way. He climbed over some rocks on the margin of the sea and then drew himself upwards by taking hold of the fern and the roots of fig trees that had penetrated the crevices; he trod softly on a ridge covered with tall grasses until he came to the recess he sought. He had to move carefully. Wolves sometimes inhabited the caves of this escarpment. He edged downwards into the dank space and lowered himself onto a ledge of rock that partially concealed the cave. Through rifts and fissures in the rock he caught glimpses of the sea, and the cave resounded with the crash of waves pounding the stone shore. Yet here he could not be seen. It was cool, not cold, and dry.

For the next few days the cave became his home, from which he made various forays for food and water. By crawling to its furthest reach, closest to the sea, he could look out from an aperture in the rock; from here he watched the white streaks that sometimes emerged upon the blue surface. Were they the traces of sea witches, or of mermaids? One morning an English patrol boat crossed the sea in front of him; it lost its speed and then turned towards the island. For a moment it seemed to be moving towards him; but he realised that it was making its way to the inlet close to his cave.

He was not alarmed because he knew that he could not be seen. It took only a moment to convince himself, however, that these were the men somehow responsible for the death of Fabio and the destruction of the farmhouse. After a few minutes he ventured outside and crept towards the inlet, just in time to see four English soldiers making their way up the path he always took to the shore.

He followed them carefully and when they turned to the left just before reaching a grove of old pine trees he knew where they were going. The surface was firmer here, kept in place by the remnants of narrow red bricks, and as he climbed upwards he could see the outline of an ancient villa with its loggia, corridors, and rooms still containing fragments of marble pavement. An old well-head lay close by among the grass and foliage. He had only come here once before, since it was known as a *male sito* that might drag you back to the time when this villa had stood intact. His parents had not known its age. It had always been here.

You could only free yourself of its grip if you ran out into the sun and climbed a further three hundred yards to the tower on the summit of the hill. This was a *torre di guardia*, built as a watch against pirates. Theo had seen them on other islands, from which the inhabitants could survey the threatening sea. This must have been why the English had come to this place.

He was kicked, and fell to the ground. As he lay sprawled in the dust he look up and saw a young soldier grinning at him. The man held out both hands, as if miming surrender, and laughed. He signalled him to get up and, as he rose, he kicked him again. Then he beckoned him to follow him. He pushed him through the entrance to the tower before shouting something. The soldier led Theo up some winding brick stairs until they reached an observation platform, with brick arches framing a number of open views. Six soldiers were standing here, two of them leaning out to gaze at the sea and the island below. The man who had taken him went up to one of his colleagues and whispered something to him. He seemed to have some remnants of authority in a beleaguered platoon.

'You, boy,' the officer said to Theo. 'Where do you live? Dove abiti?' He spoke in the dialect of northern Italy, or what Theo knew as 'baby Italian'.

'Abito qua. Su quest'isola.'

'Where is your family?'

He put up one finger. 'I live alone.'

'Good.' The officer stepped closer to him. 'Have you seen any Germans? Jerries? Huns?'

'Niente.'

'And you know the island well?'

'Certo, signore.'

'The boy understands English better than I do. Perhaps he has a teacher.' He kicked Theodore again. 'Stay away from the Germans. They will kill you. They are evil devils'. He took a coin out of his pocket, tossed it in the air and caught it. 'We will return here every week. At this time. Keep watch for any Germans. If you lead us to them, I will give you fifteen lire for each man. Do you understand?'

Theo understood well enough. He had often seeen money changing hands from soldiery to islanders. 'You're a handsome kid. Molto bello. Do you understand that?' He grabbed the boy and to the amusement of the other soldiers pretended to wrestle with him, taking care to caress his bum and private parts. Then he pulled down the boy's short trousers, and with a tin of axle grease penetrated him. 'This is what the Gemans do. And worse. Capisci?' Theo nodded but looked down at the ground. He would not look at the man who had assaulted him. He would not look at the soldiers who had killed his brother and destroyed the farmhouse. 'You can go now. But don't forget. Fifteen lire for each German.'

As soon as he left the tower he began to run down the slope into the welcoming embrace of the wild palm and the olive trees. It was at this moment that he vowed revenge on the Englishmen. He had not the slightest knowledge of how to proceed, yet this was now his island. He was alone. He needed to protect it and to preserve its honour.

On the following morning he left the cave and bathed in the clear water of the inlet. The patrol boat had gone. All around him the stone was carved into delicate shapes by the incessant motion of the waves. He threw pebbles against the face of the cliff, disturbing some rock doves. Later in the day he made his way slowly and indirectly to a stream with a bed of small white stones; in this spot he liked to sit and look out to sea. For a moment he thought he saw the wake of something rippling in the water, but it was gone.

He knew that he could never return to the farmhouse – he did not wish to imagine what he would find if he went back – and his journeys now always avoided that fixed point in his past. He went instead to quiet places, secluded places, places where the trees touched one another to form a canopy.

A few days after his encounter with the English, he climbed up to the forest of fir, beech and pine that flourished in the northern part of the island; he plunged into the sea of glittering bracken that reached up to his waist, but stopped suddenly when he saw that another track had been made. A trail of crushed and broken foliage curved between the trees, where someone had walked or run through the forest. Theodore, alerted to the presence of a stranger, stood quite still; then he ducked down in the fear that he might be seen. There was no sound except for the chirping of the cicada and the rasp of the grasshoppers.

He was still for some minutes, but nothing stirred. He stood upright, and saw nothing. The trail might have been made by a goat or a sheep that had strayed; with a new-found confidence he decided to follow the path. He walked along it through the trees, savouring the dankness of the crushed bracken, until he came to a small hollow or clearing; an area had been flattened out just at a point where a vantage could be taken of this part of the island. He noticed something on the ground that looked to him like the butt of a cigarette. As he stooped to pick it up, he heard a voice.

'Aha! Vuoi una sigaretta? Ecco qua. Prendi. Camels.' Theo turned to see a tall man standing behind him. He shook his head in reply to his question. 'Too strong? I know.' He pointed to himself. 'German.' Theo must have registered a look of shock or fear. 'I'm not the devil, you know.' Around the man's neck hung a pair of binoculars, and Theo noticed a revolver tucked into his khaki belt. 'Where is your family?'

'I am alone.'

'Are you? I am alone, too. Two alones.' This German spoke fluently the language of the region. 'Welcome.' A small tent had been erected just at the edge of the area, beneath the trees. A kettle stood on a primus stove outside the tent, together with tin cutlery and cans of food. 'No place like home,' the soldier said. He went inside the tent, and neatly folded a sleeping bag that lay crumpled on the ground. 'How old are you?'

'Thirteen. Fourteen.'

'Good to be sure. Where is your family?'

'Dead. Malaria.' He had no intention of mentioning Fabio.

'Is that so? You are a survivor then.'

'There is food and water on the island.'

'Now that's where you may be able to help me. My name is Andreas, by the way. And you?'

'Theodore.'

'A good name. Do you fancy a cup of coffee, Theodore?' He had not had a hot drink since the day before the farmhouse was destroyed. He nodded, but the soldier had already begun to light the primus stove. 'It is quiet here,' the German said as they sat together on the forest floor. 'In Sicily it was not so quiet.' He lit a cigarette and lay down, looking up at the canopy of trees. 'I can sometimes hear the bombs, on a quiet day. How did you come here?'

'I climbed through the forest, safe from hostile eyes.'

'So you know the island well.'

'Oh yes. Every part of it.'

'Have you seen any Englishmen?'

It took him only a moment to lie, and avoid any complications. 'No. You are the only foreigner. Yet you speak Italian.'

'My mother comes from Sicily.'

The morning had grown humid, so that the leaves and branches around them seemed to be bathed in moisture. 'I can't sleep at night,' the German said. 'There is no breeze.'

Yet only three days later the wind started up. It came from the south, bringing with it a veil of grey mist that crept over the hills and penetrated the crevices of the rocks; the odour of decay and dissolution rose up from the moist floor of the forest, and its carpet of vegetation, even as the beeches began to turn to gold. 'The damp is getting to me,' the soldier told Theo. 'I am aching all over. And my head hurts.' His face was drained of colour, and there was a slight tremor in his left eye. Theo brought him figs and green almonds, but the German put them aside; instead he mixed water with sugar, and drank it off in deep draughts.

On the following morning he was shivering in his sleeping bag. 'I'm not so good,' he said. Theo knew the signs from his mother and father. 'I was burning up in the night.' He was even weaker on the next day. 'The quinine doesn't help,' he said. 'It makes me sick. There is a band of Englishmen somewhere on the island, even if you have not yet seen them.'

'The English are fools. They speak freely because they do not know that I speak their language. I can understand the words from my years in Realschule. This is what I learn. They are stranded and seek means of recovery. These are six men from a small platoon in an English village called Little Camborne. Remember that place. It may be important. I want to show you something which may be connected with these men. They spoke of treasure which had been taken from this island back to England. Of course, you cannot believe soldiers' tales, but they spoke only to one another. I stole this from the sergeant I killed in the forest. It looked important.' He handed to Theo a piece of paper from a saddle-bag at the back of the tent upon which were drawn a number of squares and circles. He pointed to one of the larger circles.

'Here is their village, which they call Little Camborne. This is a field. There are figures here which may be metres or yards. Who knows? But here is a sign. An "X". I believe this is the treasure they discusssed. I cannot think what else it can be. Can you?' Theo shook his head. The soldier handed the map to the boy. 'Keep it safe. Leave it to your children, if you must. Someone will find the place one day.' Theo folded the paper and put it in the pocket of his threadbare trousers; even then he made a promise to himself that, one day, he would travel to England in order to decipher the map and exact revenge on the English devils.

He returned the following morning. The soldier now looked old. His skin was blanched, and his face drawn back. 'What typewriter do you use?' he asked the boy. 'A Royal or a Smith?' Theo did not know what he was saying. 'Everyone all right? Better get down beside the wall. Better get down.' Then he fell silent.

Theo left the forest and went back to the watchtower. 'I have found you a German,' he told the English officer. 'Can I have fifteen lire?'

Chapter 11

Goats and Dust

'Have we arrived yet? Oh dear.' As Millicent Swallow sat up she opened her eyes, to see a small crowd gathered around her. 'Where am I? Sorry. Silly question.'

'You took a tumble, dear,' Maud told her. 'And look. Here is Theodore. What a coincidence.'

'You must come into to the restaurant,' he said. 'We will give you a nice cup of tea.'

She allowed herself to be taken inside, still bewildered by her sudden loss of consciousness. 'I'm very sorry,' she said, 'to be such a nuisance.'

'Nonsense, Milly. It was just a funny turn.'

'Funny turn' sounded about right; it was a momentary lapse, a lacuna, a gap, that was without explanation. A funny turn could be seen in the theatre, or on television, and was harmless. 'I must have been light-headed for a moment.'

'It has been very hot.' Millicent put on her hat, which had come off during her fall.

'After we have enjoyed our tea, dear Miss Swallow, we will take you back to the hotel. Where you can rest.'

So they returned to the Christopher. Millicent lay upon the narrow bed, looking forlornly at the cracks in the ceiling and feeling vaguely guilty that she had not joined Maud on a sudden shopping expedition to Regent Street. But she could not bear entering the crowds, the traffic and the general air of busy activity. Somehow she connected them with her fainting fit outside the restaurant. The weight of London seemed to press upon her.

As she passed the reception she could hear Theodore and his relative talking in the small office behind it. They lowered their voices when she passed, no doubt out of sympathy for her ordeal. But she heard the word 'tesoro', and then Theodore closed the door of the reception and began talking in English. He spoke slowly to his relative. 'Niente, trees are two a penny. They prove nothing. I have found gates, trees and barns but not as the maps have it. You know, Carlo, there are too many gates and trees in this country. Troppi! And too many maps!'

'This is true.'

'But Mr Cadmus is cunning. Mr Cadmus is crafty. I will find something else. Un altro tipo di tesoro, Carlo. Un altro tipo.' Millicent did not know what the last phrase meant, but to her it sounded faintly sinister. 'Ah, Millicent, you are quite recovered.' Theo had walked into the lobby as if he had been expecting her.

'Almost. I feel a little trembly.'

'We all feel – what you say – trembly before great enterprises.'

Millicent had no idea what he meant. 'I'm a little dizzy still.'

'Nonsense. You look wildly enchanting And who is this? Maud, bearing gifts?'

Maud Finch had entered the hotel through a creaking

revolving door, clutching two green Harrods bags. She seemed faintly embarrassed. 'I have been naughty,' she said.

'We are all naughty,' Cadmus said, clapping his hand on his thigh. 'Some more than others.'

Maud took out two cellophane packages. She had purchased a luxury range of lingerie delicately labelled 'nightwear'. For a horrifying moment Millicent believed that it was something to do with Theodore's great enterprise. She was further alarmed when Theodore announced that Maud would wear the garments on this special occasion. 'I am very broad-minded. I know that ladies love silk.'

Millicent was horrified. She had an image of Maud dancing in bare feet, wearing that black negligee, in front of Theo. All she could think of was Salome, which was not wholly encouraging. Her fears were largely allayed, however, when Theo announced to the ladies, 'Carlo is preparing a feast for us in honour of Millicent. A banchetto for her miracle!'

The restaurant was a small bar and lounge on the ground floor, overlooking the street where various bins cluttered the front gardens. Carlo had put on the record player to play 'Arrivederci Roma' sung by an unknown trio and had decorated the bar with fairy lights last used at Christmas. He came in wearing a dinner jacket a size too small for him and put on extra pomade for the occasion, which made the restaurant smell like a barber's shop. 'Tonight,' he said, 'we begin with the brodo.'

'Bread?' asked Maud.

'No. Not precisely bread. And then . . .' He kissed his fingers. 'Zampetti di maiale!'

'What is that?'

'Zampetti di maiale? It is a lovely Italian specialty.'

'Meat?'

'Of course it is meat. Pigs' trotters. Ankles. Knuckles. Delicious!'

The brodo came almost at once in small blue soup-plates. It was of a pale and watery consistency, with pieces of fish floating within it. It might have tasted of celery. It might have tasted of carrot. It was hard to be sure. Maud looked at Millicent, but they said nothing. 'Can you savour the scent of the sea?' Theo asked them. 'I can feel the salt wind blow and see the sails unfurl. Ah, Italia! We are good fishermen, are we not?' Since the brodo offered no evidence either way, the women remained silent.

The next course posed more difficulty. Certain pieces of the armature of pigs seemed to have been boiled in milk that was just on the point of curdling.

'I wouldn't be surprised to see the tail,' Maud whispered. 'Like a worm.'

'Don't!'

'There doesn't seem to be much flesh here.'

Theo was indulgent to their insular tastes. 'Suck, dear Maud. Suck. The beauty is in the sucking.'

Neither Millicent nor Maud were accustomed to sucking food, and decided to pick instead. A piece of knuckle skidded off Millicent's plate and landed on the carpet.

'Allow me,' Carlo said. He washed it in water from the tap behind the bar, and replaced it on her plate. 'No harm.'

'Oh good. I would hate to waste any.'

Maud put a piece in her mouth with her fork, and began to chew on it. After an audible crunch she decided to take out the morsel and put it on the side of her plate. 'I was worried about my teeth,' she said. 'Dentures can be very expensive.'

'How is it?' Theo asked her.

'Utterly delicious. But it could have done with a tiny bit more meat.'

'You should store it up, dear Maud, like squirrels in their cheeks.'

'Oh, that would be digusting. What if somebody slapped me on the back?'

'Did I not tell you that we have a maid for little slips and indiscretions? You may remember her, Milly. Peggy was once your neighbour,' Cadmus said.

'What?'

'Everyone recommended her. Even the fireman. He called her brave. She was the one who rescued your rag-dog. I said to Carlo, we need a stalwart girl in Earl's Court.'

Millicent did not know this heroine. But she shuddered at the mention of a neighbour.

'I shall present her to you.' He rang the wine glass with a fork. The door opened and a thin woman with close-cropped hair sidled in without making a noise. She wore an appropriate expression of grief and sympathy at the loss of Milly's relatives, all those years ago.

'Is that you, Miss Milly?' she said, clasping her arms together. 'I would have known you anywhere.'

Millicent had no recollection of this woman, and the house, or the street. It even crossed her mind that she was something of a fraud. That impression was dispelled when Peggy recalled their house next door in Wellesley Street and 'the floppy hound' Millicent carried everywhere. Milly put on a brave face, all the while steeling herself for an ordeal. 'Do you remember me now?' the woman asked her.

'It's a long time ago.'

'But I never forget a face.'

'Oh how lovely.' Millicent decided to resign. 'After all this time—'

'Forty years.'

'You have a good memory.'

'How could I forget?'

'Of course.' Millicent shook her head. 'A day to remember.'

'You were the brave one,' Peggy said. 'You never cried once. It's lucky you weren't killed. When I saw you running into the garden, I knew that something was wrong. Then we saw the fire.'

'I had called the firemen, you know.'

'I know that. Of course you had.'

'But there was nothing else I could do.'

'The flames were too strong, love.'

'I told them all I knew.'

'What was it? I can't recall exactly.'

'A gas leak. The joint was faulty. I told the police everything.'

'You didn't scream. You just stood there, your arms hanging down at your sides. I remember it as if it were yesterday.'

'I didn't know what was happening. I froze.'

'No. You never showed any emotion. You were wearing a bright blue dress.'

'Was I?'

'I often wondered what happened to it.'

'I must have thrown it away. Along with the others . . .' Millicent's voice trailed off.

'The police never found out who did it, did they?'

'Nobody did it. The pipe was loose. Faulty.'

Cadmus was listening intently.

'Just one of those things,' Peggy said.

'Yes. One of those things. Wartime.'

'You were ever so brave at the coroner's.'

'Was I?' All she remembered clearly was the wooden rail she clutched while everyone was talking around her. She sensed vaguely that she was being pitied, and her resentment heightened the colour of her cheeks. *She* felt no pity. Death by misadventure. Some misadventure. Was that what it was? She smelled the wax polish on the long table in front of her, and had a sudden almost overwhelming desire to comb her hair. But that would be indiscreet and reflect badly upon her. She waited until the coroner and jury had left the court before she took out her comb.

'You were very brave,' Peggy said. 'You spoke out in such a clear voice.' (This is what Milly had said: *I smelled gas and then I called to them. I think the hot plate was on. There was a fire.*) 'Where did you go afterward?'

'My auntie looked after me.'

'I saw you walk away by yourself after the funeral.'

'I didn't know where I was. I was poorly for a time, and then I got better.'

'Is that when your auntie took you in? She lived in Ealing, didn't she?'

'That's when I changed school. That's when I got the idea of being a nurse.'

'Is that what you are now, Milly?'

'I was. I retired. The patients were getting on my nerves. The sick can be very nasty.'

'Still, you seem very cheerful now.'

'I get by, Peggy.'

'Still waiting for that special person?'

'Oh, I gave that up years ago. The right man must be long gone. Oh dear. I think I still need a little air.'

'Let me get you an aspirin,' Maud said. 'There's a chemist on the other side of the road.'

Maud got up from the table to leave.

'I'll get some elastoplast too,' she told Millicent. 'You have a cut on your chin.'

'Am I bloody?'

'It's just a little nick, but nicks can grow. You will look like Lady Macbeth.'

Maud said goodbye to Peggy and left. But Peggy accompanied her across the road. Millicent believed that here was an opportunity to change the conversation.

'I hope I didn't upset you when I fainted.'

'Not in the least,' Theo said. 'It was perfectly all right. It was a hot day, dear Miss Swallow. It could have happened to anyone.'

'But I felt such a fool. With all that crowd around me.'

'But you are not a fool, Millicent.'

'No. I am not.'

'You are very observant. The eyes in the back of the head.'

'I would not go so far, Theo. But I do try and keep my wits about me.' They were silent for a moment. 'But what has happened to Carlo?' she asked Theo. 'He became invisible after the second course. And that reminds me. Did we not see you in that restaurant with him? The one who looks like a gigolo. The one who just served us.'

'He is not a gigolo, Millicent.' Theodore did not approve of her tone. 'He is a receptionist from Rome.'

'I just said he looked like one. Looking is not being.'

'He was not with me, dear lady. I was alone.'

'That is peculiar. I could swear that he was there,' she replied. 'And another man. It's all very confusing.'

'You were agitated, Milly,' Theo said. 'The mind plays little tricks. It's only natural. But please, tell me how you are enjoying your time back in London.'

'It's changed so much, I feel like a stranger.'

Theo listened for a while but then became bored and said, 'I wonder where dear Maud has got to?'

As if he had summoned her, Maud appeared in front of the restaurant clutching a bottle. 'It was rude of me to delay you further,' she said. 'But after I went to the chemist I bought this in memory of our meal.'

'Ah,' Theo exclaimed. 'Grappa!'

'I was told it was from your island.' Maud was opening the bottle with some difficulty. 'But I can never remember the island's name. It must be enchanted.'

'Caldera,' Millicent said with a hint of impatience.

'I looked it up on a map, but I couldn't see it.'

'Should you not wear reading glasses, dear? Everything will be much clearer.'

'It is very small,' Theodore said. 'Insignificant.'

'But surely you have happy memories of it?' Millicent asked him. 'Childhood is happy.'

'Not always,' Maud muttered.

'Goats and dust. That is all.' They walked back to the hotel.

'Let's drink to them,' Maud said. 'To goats and dust.'

'No, no,' Theo said. 'We must forget about them.'

They were interrupted by the arrival of Carlo carrying a plate of what looked to Maud like doughnuts soaked in syrup. Millicent gazed at them eagerly. 'Rum baba! I thought they came from France.'

'I thought it was a dance,' Maud said.

'We also make them in southern Italy,' Theo told them. 'Where the oranges grow.'

The two ladies, starved after the first two courses, ate them greedily and quickly.

'You ladies must now try our very special drink.' Carlo came back from behind the counter. 'It is made for rum baba.'

'Don't tell me it is rum.' Millicent pursed her lips.

'No, no. Limoncello. Made at home. Christopher-style.' From behind the bar he brought out a a bottle of what looked like custard. 'Very sweet, like ladies' lips. Very sour, like ladies' tongues.'

'I don't think that's quite the right way of putting it,' she replied.

'It is our only night in London, ladies. Surely we are allowed to be a little bit bad?' Theo looked at them with gleaming eyes. 'I may even tell you a secret when we are back home.'

Chapter 12

A Conniption Fit

'I have found so many secrets in this village,' the deaconess was telling Mr Cadmus, 'that someday I might burst.'

'If you choose any spot on earth, reverend lady—'

'June.'

'You will find mysteries. The heart can be deceitful. I have known some strange events in Caldera.'

'Let me show you this, Mr Cadmus. It is what we call a parish register. We keep the details of all our parishioners here. Birth. Marriage.'

'Death.' He still distrusted June.

'Yes, of course. But there are other details pasted in for general interest. And that was when I thought of your special interest. Look here, at the entry of 12 May 1945. Four days after the war had ended. Forgive me for bringing up such sad events.'

'Not at all. On the island all is one.'

'Do you see there? "The Little Camborne Regiment, sadly depleted after enemy action, took refuge on the island of Caldera." I came across it quite by accident. What do you make of it?'

Theo thought for a moment, with his eyes closed. 'It is one of those wonderful coincidences that bring us together, dear lady. Now I feel very close to you. Spiritually.'

'And here is the interesting part. It refers to all the soldiers who survived.'

'Oh indeed?' He was burning with hate. They were the men who had shot his brother.

'There were six of them. We treat them as heroes.'

'Of course. It is quite natural. Are the names written here also?'

'Oh yes. Here is dear old Cunningham, the lieutenant. And there, look, is Denny. Wesley. Deacon. And the two Appleby brothers.'

'They are still with us, I believe.'

'Oh yes. In roaring health. There have been casualties, Denny and Deacon have passed away, unfortunately. But Cunningham is still active.'

'And what about the sixth man you mentioned?'

'Wesley? He is a little poorly, I'm afraid, but he is in good spirits.'

'And they would never leave Little Camborne.'

'Oh God, no. They wouldn't budge.'

'I would so like to thank them for saving my beloved island.'

'I am sure that can be arranged. They are in the same cottages as they once were and would be delighted to meet a fellow combatant. Did you actually join them, Mr Cadmus?'

'Oh no. That was not possible. The Germans . . .'

'I see. Keep the Jerry guessing. But now, after all these years, you can meet in perfect harmony.'

'That is one of the reasons I came to Little Camborne. To be reunited with old comrades! It is time to look up old friends, don't you think? Lest old remembrance be forgot?'

'Would you like a general reunion? In the village hall?'

'No, no. Something discreet. Like me, these older men have strong emotions of the past.'

'Of course. I will leave it to you.'

'I think it best that I introduce myself. So that they may recognise me more easily.' He did not come to commiserate with his brother's killers. 'You said that Wesley was poorly. Do you know his ailment?'

'Circulation. Sluggish circulation.'

'Oh dear me, I know it all. My island is very hot and very still. We have herbs.'

He was seen by Millicent the next morning carrying a wicker basket of foxgloves and buttercups with which he proceeded into his kitchen. Maud heard the sounds of pounding and scraping, with an occasional muttered phrase. She went to his kitchen door. 'Can I help?'

'Dear Miss Finch, this is an old recipe. Here. Taste it. It is perfectly harmless.' Reluctantly she sipped the brown liquor with a teaspoon. It must have been the weather, she said later, but she felt giddy in what she described as 'a pleasant sort of way'. 'Oh, I must get some,' she said.

'No, dear Miss Finch. This is only for special cases.'

'Your country medicines seem far superior to our own.'

'Let us see.'

After Theodore Cadmus paid him a visit, John Wesley did seem to revive for a day or so, but then with no apparent warning slipped into a deep slumber that preceded death. Mr Cadmus held deep discussions with the country doctor, who agreed with his diagnosis of sluggish blood. It was not unknown even in Little Camborne, but the talk of consulting a specialist in Dorchester was considered to be unnecessary.

★

'I must visit Lieutenant Cunningham,' Mr Cadmus said after the funeral. 'An old colleague may comfort him.'

The next day, he tapped on the lieutenant's door. 'May I come in?'

'Who the hell are you?' Cunningham snapped. He had not seen Cadmus at the funeral.

'I am an old friend.'

'I don't have any old friends.'

'All dead?'

'What business is it of yours?'

'More than you may imagine, Lieutenant Cunningham.'

'Come into the light.'

'If you do not recognise me, perhaps you will know this.' He held up the piece of paper which the German had confided to him before the soldier's death. It was the map which Cadmus had not been able to decipher.

Cunningham peered at it, and was puzzled.

'It is the paper stolen from one of your men who was killed in the forest,' said Cadmus.

'Bianco. He was the map-reader.'

'You believed in treasure to be found here.'

'So you are a thief!' Cunningham barked.

'And you treated me like one. Do you remember shooting my brother? Do you remember burning down our farmhouse? And raping me? Oh yes, you have a lot to remember.'

'How dare you question me? How dare you?'

'I dare. And I dare to tell this quaint little village what you did to me.'

Cunningham stood up in his chair but then slumped backwards with a sigh; his tongue protruded from his mouth with a life all its own and his face was contorted.

Cadmus ran to the house next door and asked for the

doctor. 'Our brave lieutenant is having a stroke. Please be as quick as you can.'

The doctor knew the signs. 'A conniption fit. Common among old soldiers. Make him comfortable with some blankets.'

'Will he survive?' Theo asked the doctor impatiently.

'At his age it is not likely. The conniption fit is the most fatal. The consequences of war can linger for several years.'

'What could have caused it?' the neighbour asked.

'A sudden shock is most likely.'

'But he and I,' Cadmus said, 'were talking of old times and happy memories. He was very cheerful."

'Then he has a blessed death. But the sudden memory of old times may cause something like a brainstorm.'

There was no need for the presence of Mr Cadmus for this simple death, and he went back to the Coppice in a cheerful mood.

He adopted a more severe expression when Millicent Swallow rushed out of the door. 'Three deaths, is it?' she asked him in her excitement. 'Denny, Deacon and now Cunningham.'

'I am afraid so.'

'Are we cursed?'

'Only with old age, Millicent.'

'And did you know them?'

'No. On our island we did not mix with any of the soldiers. But I told you ladies in London that I had a secret, did I not?'

'I can't wait.'

'No, we must wait for Maud. She went to Dorchester for her magazines.'

'She cannot exist without *Woman's Own*,' said Millicent. 'Or the horoscopes.'

'She should not read them. On our island they are scorned.'

'But Eileen Watson swears by them. Won't go an inch without them.'

'What nonsense, Millicent. Ah, here is Maud with all the news.'

'And now you can tell us your secret.' Millicent looked expectantly at Cadmus.

'Let us go inside.' He led them into his front parlour where Isolde was grooming her feathers. She stopped as soon as she saw the ladies. 'Knees up, Mother Brown,' she crooned, 'Knees up, Mother Brown. Under the table you must go, ee-aye, ee-aye, ee-aye oh.'

'At least her vocabulary is less appalling,' Maud said. The parrot gave her a baleful glance.

Chapter 13

Green Fingers

'Now,' Theo said. 'I have something secret to show you. It is a very secret thing. Carlo does not think it wise to display it. But I trust you ladies with my life.' He went into the kitchen and came back with a piece of paper that he carefully laid down on the dining room table. It was the map he had shown to Cunningham.

'There is nothing secret about it,' Maud said. 'It's a map of North Devon.' She peered at it for a few seconds. 'There's Little Camborne. Just a dot.'

'Do you see the pencil marks leading from it?'

'To the "X" sign? Of course. I don't know what it means. At a guess, it marks a piece of somebody's land.'

'I have been there,' Theo said. 'Just a field of grass only.'

'What do you expect? The Taj Mahal?'

'Wait, ladies. I have another piece of paper.' He took a folded sheet from his top pocket, and smoothed it out on the table. 'What to make of this?'

'I make nothing of it,' Maud replied.

'It looks like someone has drawn a hill,' Millicent said.

'With a tree on top of it. That jagged thing next to it might be a rock.'

'And the round thing?' he asked her.

'A pond?'

'It looks,' Maud said, 'as if it has been drawn by a child. No, it is not a pond. It is in a singular shape.'

'A good friend gave it to me. He says it is somewhere close to our village.'

'Your good friend was mistaken,' Maud told him.

'He was very sick. Feverish. He died on Caldera before I could question him.'

Maud studied the scrawled hill and tree. 'Well, there is no such area.'

'Just wait a minute.' They looked at Millicent. 'You will think I'm mad.' They still waited. 'What about Burrow Hill?'

'Oh that old chestnut.' Maud was unimpressed.

'Chestnut?' Theo asked them. 'What is this?'

'An old story,' Maud told him.

'Not that old. I heard it from my hairdresser. You know, Mrs Killigew from Hairspace who preceded dear Maurice.'

'Please to go on, dear Millicent.'

'Well, Maud is right in one sense. It is an old story. There is a hill, with a tree and a rock. And there is a pond, although it must have dried up by now. But it's nowhere near this.' She pointed at the pencil marks. 'It is in Little Molton?'

'It doesn't fit, Millicent.'

'But, Maud, the drawing does look like the little rock.' She looked at Theo. 'That rock goes back millions of years.'

'Oh don't be ridiculous, Milly. Nothing here goes back millions of years. Except the ice cream.'

'It is very nice ice cream,' Millicent replied.

'My ladies, please tell me about the hill.'

'As I said, there is a story.'

'But what is it?' Theo was becoming impatient.

'We all know here of the black stone of Burrow Hill. No one could move it. They tried everything. I'm talking about the Fifties. Drills. Spades. Pitchforks. Cranes. Claw hammers. Nothing worked on the black stone. Not even dynamite, about which the villagers were very annoyed. It seemed like sacrilege.'

'And so?' Theo asked.

'All sorts of stories started up. We have a mine of supernatural legends, as you know, Mr Cadmus.'

'Yes, I have heard of your hobs and ghosts and dobies. It is the same on Caldera.'

'But this is the unbelievable part.'

'I thought so,' Maud said, who distrusted Mrs Killigrew from Hairspace.

Millicent ignored her and continued: 'One of those German rockets hit the stone square on. A doodlebug, was it called?'

'V–1?' Cadmus suggested.

'V-something,' Millicent replied. 'What a racket it made! But that isn't the end of the story. On the following day the black stone was nowhere to be seen. And there in its place was an amethyst! As large as a golf ball.'

So here, Cadmus thought, *is the story of the treasure.*

'What happened to the miraculous jewel?' he asked Millicent.

'The soldiers took it. They said that they were the lawful authority. It vanished. Or got stolen. But everyone still talks of the missing amethyst.'

Mr Cadmus, ever more mysterious, took out another paper from his wallet. 'My friend caught sight of it once and recalled it instantly. He was a trained observer. And this is it.' He turned the paper over and on the other side of a small map there was a drawing which might have been a rough approximation to a precious stone, with its striated patches and jagged edges.

'Why did your friend draw the jewel?' Maud asked Theo.

'Perhaps he wanted to tell the story. He was very sick.'

'He might have wanted you to find it.'

'Yes,' Theo said. 'He dearly wanted that. It is my greatest wish to follow his path. I know that he would have wished to donate the jewel to our local church.' Maud looked horrified. 'Under different auspices, of course, than the present St Leonard's.'

'Would you like us to go with you?' Millicent had amethysts in her eyes.

'It will be dirty and messy, dear lady.'

'But exciting,' Millicent said. 'Like a treasure hunt.'

'Except,' Maud replied, 'there is generally treasure in a treasure hunt.'

'I doubt there will be treasure,' Theo said.

'So what's the point?' Maud asked him.

'No point for the ladies. No point at all. I go there in memory of my distressed friend. That is all. I go to shed a tear. What is it your poet says? A piece of field. For ever England. A tear for ever.'

'I think it is a wonderful idea,' Millicent said. 'To mark the spot where a bomb created a beautiful stone.' Millicent was more interested in the beautiful stone than the bomb. 'It could have been buried there as bad luck, to prevent robbers. We often read of explorers putting their discoveries back before dying.'

Mr Cadmus looked steadily at her. 'That was precisely my theory, dear Miss Swallow. Why else would it disappear so completely on the very spot it appeared? Just a few ignorant soldiers who would not know emeralds from green glass.' He took out a handkerchief and wiped his forehead. 'Well, ladies, shall we say goodnight? We must be early birds who catch the worms.'

They caught the early morning train from Barnstaple, and on the first part of the journey to their destination at Little Molton, Theo Cadmus remained deep in the solution of a crossword that seemed to be causing him much irritation. 'Who,' he asked aloud, 'is Lord Peter Wimsey?'

'He is a very brilliant detective,' Millicent told him. 'He specialises in murders. Especially of old women.'

'He is a real person?'

'Oh Lord, no. He is made up. Like Sherlock Holmes. The fictional detectives are always the best. Like fictional murders. Much more satisfying.'

'What am I supposed to do with this clue? "Lord Peter Wimsey cannot measure the dose. Eight letters."'

'Well,' Maud said, 'it's obviously a poison. Did you say eight letters? Laudanum.'

'But I must get there from here.' He tapped the page of the newspaper. 'It is a leap I cannot make. There are two "M"s which do not fit. I can't get to a poison.'

'What about good old morphine?' Maud asked him.

'Only one "M".'

'I know,' Millicent said. 'Methomyl. Doesn't leave a trace.'

'How do you know that?' Maud asked her.

'Nursing training.'

'But it has nothing to do with our clue,' Theo said. 'Or with Lord Peter Wimsey.'

'He was in a book called *Five Red Herrings*.' Millicent looked out of the window, as if certain of her solution. 'And *that* was to do with a poisoning.'

Theo flung the newspaper to the other side of the compartment. 'You ladies have your heads filled with poisons.'

On the second part of their journey fom Swinderbury to Little Molton, he looked keenly out of the window of the slow local train, scrutinising the landscape as if it were hostile territory. 'There's a hill,' he said. 'And there's another one.' He leaned forward in his seat. 'There's a tree.'

'You will not find Burrow Hill here,' Maud told him. 'It is in another county.'

'But I can never be sure. My friend may have meant some other place. Look at that! A hill with a forest across it!'

'Your friend drew a single tree, not a wood.'

'But so much is similar.'

'Trees are very similar en masse.'

'Theo, it is no good. You will have to allow us to drive you there. In your lovely car which reminds us of a banana.' Maud tapped him on the knee. 'Otherwise you will never find it.'

'Perhaps . . .'

'We are not going to steal your treasure.'

'But careless talk . . .'

'And who, precisely, are we going to tell?'

'Little Camborne is all ears, Maud,' Theo replied.

In the summer twilight the cattle cast long shadows over the grass. The sun was setting as they arrived at Little Camborne station and both ladies were looking forward to a cup of tea before bedtime. They parted company by the gates of the cottages; Millicent unlocked the door and walked into her hallway with relief, where she was profusely welcomed by Timothy. The cat purred and rubbed itself against her left leg.

About an hour later she saw Theo tapping on the window. 'I have come to a decision,' he said as he entered her kitchen. 'I need your feminine intuition. Your je ne sais quoi.'

'You want us to lead you to Burrow Hill. Is that it?'

'Exactly.'

He knocked on Maud's door a few minutes later. 'May I borrow you for a moment, Maud?' She came into the front garden. 'May I suggest a journey?'

'But we have just arrived home.'

'Indeed. But this is to somewhere much closer, Maud. Closer to to my heart.'

'Oh dear.' She tucked away a piece of hair that was threatening to come loose.

'To Burrow Hill.'

'I might have guessed,' she said.

'Frankly there was a time when I intended to keep everything to myself.'

'Keep *what* to yourself?' Maud asked him.

'The secret.'

On this note they prepared for the journey to Burrow Hill.

Chapter 14

The Line

The small yellow car made its way through the deep-set hedges on the border of Devon and Dorset. 'Napoleonic,' Maud said. No one paid any attention. 'They were built by prisoners-of-war.'

'I was a prisoner-of-war,' Theo told her. 'As a boy.'

'On that lovely little island?'

'Only for a short time. But the English taught me electrical engineering. It was invaluable.'

'I'm glad we were of some use,' Maud murmured.

'Look. There is the soldiers' castle.' Millicent was pointing to a large hill with a circle of flattened grass around its base. 'Iron Age, I think. But all those periods run into one another, don't they? At least they do for me.'

'Many of them,' Maud said, 'would have existed at the same time. Time is not linear. Now you take a right, Theo, as if you were going to Madely. Then take this next right sign to Rivercorn.' She had an Ordnance Survey on her lap, but looked up as they passed a pond fringed by yew trees. 'That looks like a magic circle.'

'I wonder,' Millicent asked, 'if I dived into the water, would I disappear?'

'What would we do without you?' Cadmus asked her.

'Oh, you would both manage, I dare say.'

There was a silence inside the car.

'I think,' Maud said, 'that we are almost there. We just passed a Burrow Hill Farm.'

'Let our eyes be peeled.' Theo leaned against the steering wheel and began to drive more slowly, turning right and left as the lane followed its route through the fields. Yet they seemed to get nowhere. 'I'm sure we passed that horse before,' Maud said. 'Or was it that one over there? Horses are not my strong point.'

'This is becoming a labyrinth.' Millicent was gleeful. 'Like a snake with its tail in its mouth.'

'It may be the first occasion,' Theo said, 'when you experience infinity.'

He stopped the engine and lowered his window. All was quiet, except for a slight rustle of the wind among the trees and grasses. 'You see,' he said, 'we are in the eye.'

'The eye of the storm?' Maud asked him.

'No. The eye of the land.'

'I don't think the land has eyes.'

'If we walk,' Millicent said, 'we might come upon Burrow Hill unawares.'

'I don't see the logic of that,' Maud replied; but she followed as Theo opened a gate and began to cross a field.

'What has logic to do with infinity? Be careful of rabbit holes,' Millicent called out.

They walked in single file, wavering this way or that for no apparent reason. They came to a slope that led down to a narrow stream. 'Did you hear voices?' Millicent asked.

'It must be the water,' Maud replied. 'It often sounds like someone whispering.'

'Ah!' Theo was striding ahead. 'There it is! The hill! And do you see the tree?!'

The two ladies looked in the direction Theo was pointing and, sure enough, on the horizon there seeemed to be a hill. 'Are you sure,' Maud asked him, 'that it is your particular one? The countryside is full of hills. It is known for them.'

'We can't possibly walk to it,' Millicent said. 'It must be miles away.'

'We will drive. We will fix it with our stares. It will draw us forward.'

'Not if we run out of petrol,' Maud said.

To her astonishment Theo took a rosary out of his trouser pocket and waved it in the air.

'It comes in handy, I suppose,' Millicent whispered to Maud. 'Like a Swiss army knife. But isn't he relying on the wrong gods? The new priest, Father Gregory, is hardly likely to approve.'

'Gregory seems to approve of anything. He is very wide. Apparently he went to an American theological college in California.'

'No!'

'That is why he has ended up in Little Camborne.'

Theo came back to the car and they set off in the general direction of the hill that he had seen, sometimes going along mud tracks or what looked like private paths. But, still, they were not stopped. The hill remained in sight, and the tree upon it at last became recognisable as an oak. A path stopped about two hundred yards away.

'At last,' he said, 'I am happy!' He left the car again and began to run forward. 'We may be the first!'

'I doubt that very much,' Maud said.

Theo was already climbing the mound. 'There is the stone,' he shouted out. 'The sacred stone he mentioned!'

'Pay no attention,' Maud told Millicent.

'If I can find a stone to fill this gap. Do you see it?' There was an indentation in the rock, the size of a penny coin. 'Then we may find my friend's hiding place.'

'This is pure hocus pocus,' Maud said. 'This is Devon, not Calabria.' They both clambered to the top, where Theo was eagerly examining the ground between the stone and the tree. Suddenly he stopped and remained very still.

'Now what is that noise, please?'

They all stood, and gazed at each other. 'I hear chatter,' Millicent said. 'And are there footsteps?'

Just as she said this, a line of walkers came into view on the brow of an inclined path which approached the hill from a southern route. 'What does this mean?' Theo asked them. They heard the sound of laughter. 'We must stay calm, ladies. We are not in the Iron Age.'

'They are in good spirits, at least,' Maud said.

'I do not think, Maud, that they are about to attack us. But what are they doing here?'

The leader of the walkers, a young man, stopped at the bottom of the hill. 'You got here just before us. Good timing.'

'Yes,' Theo replied. 'I suppose so.'

'Why are you here?' Maud suddenly asked the young man.

'Same reason as you. Following the line. It comes from Chichester. But you know that.'

'Oh, the line,' Millicent said. She had not the faintest idea what he meant.

'Of course,' the young man said. 'What other line could it be?'

Theo turned to the women. 'What is he talking about?'

'No doubt something spiritual,' Maud said.

'In Devon? Have they found anything?'

'Have you been here before?' Maud asked the young man.

'Oh yes. Many times. There's not a square inch of Burrow Hill we don't know.'

Theo was suddenly depressed. 'Ask them if they have found anything.'

'Have you found anything?'

'Where, precisely?'

'Inside the hill.'

'Not a thing. Just earth.'

'And in the neigbourhood?'

'There's nothing here.'

'A barren hill,' Theo said, 'like a barren woman.'

Maud turned to Millicent. 'It's getting rather windy here, don't you think?'

'Yes. It is chilly.'

'The cold air will do us good,' Theo told them, as the three left the hikers and headed back to the car. 'It will blow away illusions. There was no treasure or, if there was, it has already been taken.'

The journey back to Little Camborne procceded mainly in silence. Millicent dozed at the back of the car, with faint murmurs that irritated Maud intensely.

'Whatever does she mean?'

'That is one thing we will never know. I hope I do not talk in my sleep.'

'Why not?'

He put his finger to his lips. 'If we cannot speak out loud about certain things, then we must remain silent.'

They had arrived in their side-street, and the parking of the car woke Millicent.

'I'm desolate for tea,' Maud said.

'I'll make some, dear.'

'None for me, ladies. I must think over the events of the day.'

'It must have come as an awful disappointment,' Millicent said as the two women entered her sitting room. As it happened, Theo could hear every word they spoke. Some time ago he had drilled a tiny hole into the intervening wall, well camouflaged by the wooden outwork of a cuckoo clock, and by putting a glass to the hole he could hear perfectly.

'Theo was sure that he would find something,' said Maud.

'Let me get the tea,' Millicent said.

She came back a few minutes later, and Theo heard the rattling of cups and saucers.

'Well, Maud, it's all over now.'

'What is all over?

'Theo is smitten.'

'What do you mean?

'He's fallen.'

'Don't be absurd.' Maud was smiling. 'So what's all over? You are the most nonsensical woman in the world, Millicent. Now I must really get to bed. It's been a long day.'

'But a fruitful one perhaps.'

That night there was a distant rumble that might have been thunder, but was heard only by Sidney and the livestock on the Appleby farm.

Chapter 15

The Cat and the Parrot

It had been raining heavily, but Maud and Theo were busy in their gardens; Millicent watched them from the window as they seemed to be engaged in desultory conversation across the low wooden fence. If she tried hard enough Millicent could hear stray phrases – 'and then?', 'do you think?', 'what if?', 'it doesn't matter' – come and go with the damp wind.

She was surprised when Theo vaulted over the fence into Maud's garden. But he stumbled on an old root, fell forward, and slid across the mud on his knees towards her. Milly could not resist the opportunity of opening the window. 'Are you all right, Theo?'

'I slipped.'

Still on his knees he looked up at Maud, and said something which Millicent could not hear.

Maud suddenly became flustered. 'Oh do get up, Theo. It's very undignified.' He struggled to his feet. 'Just look at your trousers.'

'I shall have to take them off.'

'Not here you won't.'

'Did you hear what I said to you?'

'Very well, thank you.'

'And what is your answer?"

'My answer is to change your trousers.'

With her window open Millicent heard all of the exchange, and fretted. What on earth did it mean? What was the question and what was the answer?

Maud and Millicent attended church on the following Sunday. Theo drove them but refused to take part in the service in the presence of the deaconess. He sat in the car and waited as the high tremulous voices quivered to a close. As the organ sounded the deaconess proceeded down the aisle to the church porch where, as she said, she felt more motherly, greeting and saying goodbye.

The congregation left the church, buzzing around June like contented bees. 'And here,' she announced, 'is our new doctor for the parish. Meet Sheila.'

Sheila was a tall woman with straggling grey hair that acted as a dim halo for her earnest expresssion. She was introduced to Maud by June. The deaconess seemed to have taken over the festivities.

'How do you do, doctor?'

'Oh, no formalities, please. I'm just Sheila. Sheila Burton.' She took Maud by the elbow and squeezed it. 'I can tell there is nothing wrong with you.'

'Oh no?' Maud seemed faintly disappointed.

Sheila turned to Millicent. 'You keep a cat.'

'I do.'

'It is an irritant to your eyes. Don't let it lick your face.' This was a surprise to Millicent, who allowed Timothy to do little else.

The doctor turned back to the deaconess. 'When I see patients of a certain age, I always ask the same question.' It was not clear whether she included Maud and Millicent in that category. 'How long do you want to live?'

'But surely,' Millicent said, 'as long as possible?'

Sheila had a harsh laugh. 'Some people want to get it over with as soon as possible.'

'Why?'

'Misery.'

'Oh.'

'And there's no cure for that. Excuse me. I must scratch.' She rubbed vigorously between her legs. 'Of course you can't put them down, much as I would like to sometimes. But I don't waste expensive medicines on them. I prescribe them to people like June, a deaconess beyond all others. You see she has a passion for life. She gorges on it. She laps it up. I believe she prolongs it.'

'That doesn't sound,' Gregory said, 'very Christian.'

'Christian, Mohammedan, Gay Liberation Front, it doesn't matter. Some have got it, and some haven't. And do you know what "it" is? Inner toughness. Look at you, June. Bursting tits. Big meaty thighs.' The congregation was eager to hear every word. 'You were put on this earth to win. Am I right?'

'Well, not exactly, Sheila. I do have my church duties. Which reminds me,' June said, desperate to avert the topic of conversation, 'the annual fete is almost upon us.' There was an expectant silence among the congregation, not untouched by silent dread. It meant that money would have to be spent. 'I trust Betty will take on the teddy bear tombola and, as always, we cannot do without Mrs Trilb's chutney. I know that Jennifer Pound will lend a hand to the lucky dip, and a little bird tells me that one or two of you have been having a competition about ships in bottles. The Appleby brothers will be setting up their merry-go-round which, I gather, was such a success last year.' Any hint of the reverend

Tony was omitted. 'You'll also be delighted to hear that the Barnstable Ragtime Band have offered their services. The committee have agreed that all proceeds should go to the Spastics Society, a worthy cause I hope you'll agree. So come on, everybody, get weaving.'

Theodore wound down the window of the car. 'Excuse me, ladies, I must stretch the legs.'

Theo came out of the car and took long strides around the churchyard. Sheila looked at him approvingly. 'Good flowing motion.'

'He used to keep goats,' Millicent told her, 'on the mountains.'

'Did he? I would like to prod his patella.'

Theo came up to them, and Maud turned to him. 'The doctor here – this is Sheila, Theo – would like to prod you.'

'I am at your service, doctor Sheila.'

'Did you know,' she said, 'that goat shit can be used as a medicine?'

Sidney came up to them. 'It's true. My grandma told me that its smell could wake the dead.'

The ladies were not altogether comfortable with the conversation, and at this point June wandered in the direction of another parishioner. 'And it can, of course,' the doctor said, 'be used in certain poisons.'

'Is that so?' Theo seemed very interested. 'May I ask how you know that?'

'I did my thesis on toxicology.'

'Is it true,' Millicent asked her, 'that some poisons are undetectable?'

'Almost so. Arsenic is very difficult to trace.'

'Arsenic? Isn't that a little old-fashioned?' Maud rummaged in her handbag for her handkerchief. 'It always used to be mentioned in detective novels.'

'It works. You look a little pasty, dear, if you don't mind my saying so. Anything wrong in the nether regions?'

Maud shook her head. 'Of course not.'

'I don't suppose you have a man, do you? That would do the trick.'

Maud glared at her. 'That is the last thing on my mind.'

'Well, come round to the surgery and I'll buck you up with some iron. Nothing like it. Keeps the stools firm and moist.'

'I'm afraid,' Millicent said, 'that we must be getting back. It's been lovely meeting you.'

On the drive home Maud remained silent for a while. 'Wild horses,' she eventually said, 'would not drag me to that woman's surgery. The nerve. What would she know about men?'

'You don't mean—' Millicent ventured.

'All I will say is that she has very large hands. Even for a doctor.'

They drove back to the Coppice, Theo humming some unknown tune until he parked in the cobbled driveway in front of the three cottages. Maud had had time only to hang up her cloche hat when there came a loud shriek from the house of Theo Cadmus. She rushed into the front garden, just as Millicent hurried out; they looked at one another in consternation and called for him. He flung his door wide open and stood on the threshold. 'Isolde has been barbarously murdered. Look and weep.' He led the ladies into the front room. 'There – there – is the body.' The parrot lay on the carpet, its body having been ripped open. The cage had fallen to the floor, and there were feathers everywhere. 'No worse,' he cried, 'there is none.'

'Whatever could have happened?'

'It might have been a fox, Maud.'

'How could a fox get in?' They both went to the kitchen door, which was safely locked. 'Gloria must have left a window open.'

'Oh look.' Millicent went over to one of the kitchen windows that was ajar. She was already thinking of Timothy. 'Anything could have got through it. Even a dog.'

'I don't think dogs attack parrots, dear.'

'Terriers are capable of anything.' She knew that Maud was also thinking of Timothy.

Theodore Cadmus was weeping in the front room. 'She had a beautiful soul,' he said when they came in to comfort him. 'She was beyond price. And such a sweet voice.' Maud and Millicent looked at one another. 'I could listen to her for hours. The way she called my name – Theo, Theo – was music to me. Who could have committed this terrible crime?' He looked at Millicent.

'It could have been anyone,' she said. 'The world is a dangerous place.'

'I do not accuse Timothy, Miss Swallow. He is a cat above all others. Beyond reproach. Is he at home?'

'Oh yes. He has not been out of the house.' She had a sudden vision of the cat-flap in the kitchen door.

'He is still spotless then. Some devilish creature has murdered Isolde. I cannot look at her. He rushed into the kitchen and brought out a small table cloth that he flung over the bird. 'There. Let this be her shroud. Sleep well, Isolde.'

'Where are you going to put it?' Maud asked him.

'She shall be decently buried. In the garden.'

On the following morning Theo summoned them to the ceremony. He greeted them in a black suit and, to the ladies' amazement, a black Homburg. As they stood on the small terrace they could hear the sound of Brahms coming from Theo's gramophone. He had already dug a hole, between the rose bush and the path. Isolde was still wrapped in the table cloth and, with great dignity, he placed the bundle in the earth. He took a Catholic missal out of the pocket of his jacket, raised his eyes and muttered some words that neither Maud nor Millicent could understand. When he paused they both intoned 'Amen'.

'That was,' Millicent said to Maud later that day, 'a very nice service. Very moving.'

'It was only a dead bird.'

'Nevertheless it was all very sad and dignified. Under the circumstances.'

Timothy seemed to be off his food over the next few days. Millicent offered him little delicacies such as lamb's heart and calves' liver, but the cat turned away. It hid itself in corners, and crept under Millicent's bed. And then it vanished; it was nowhere to be seen. Over the next few days, at twilight, Millicent stood at the bottom of her garden calling out in a high voice 'Timothy! Timothy!!'

'I think,' she said to Maud one evening as they sat in Maud's kitchen, 'that he has gone into the woods. I think he left out of guilt.'

'Guilt?'

'For Isolde.' She leaned over to her and whispered. 'I think he did it. But don't tell Theo. It would upset him too much.'

'Timothy was always the likely suspect.'

'He realised that he had done wrong, and was ashamed. That's the only explanation I can think of. He was very sensitive.'

'I don't think cats behave like that, Millicent.'

'Oh, you don't know them as well as I do. They were worshipped in Egypt, weren't they? They have great powers of comprehension.'

'Are you sure?'

'I saw it in his eyes after Isolde's funeral. If he could have blushed, he would have done.' Maud looked down into her cup. 'Animals,' Millicent continued, 'are very susceptible, you know. Very sensitive.'

When the front doorbell rang Millicent got up eagerly, as if Timothy himself was at the door. She came back into the kitchen with Theo, who took off the black Homburg hat he was wearing. 'Any news, Miss Swallow?'

'None whatsoever.'

'Perhaps he has been kidnapped. Abducted.'

'What person in their right mind would do such a thing?'

'There are evil people in the world, dear Miss Swallow, who stop at nothing.'

'I hope I never meet one.'

'But how would you know?' he asked her.

'I have a sixth sense about such things.'

'Really?'

'One touch would tell me.'

'Well.' He put his hand upon her arm. 'You see that I am a good person.'

Chapter 16

The Gypsy

'We were thinking of driving into Dorchester,' Maud said to Millicent a few days later. 'Theo wants to dig up Isolde and get her stuffed. Then we can have a scone in the tea-room.'

'Is that wise?' Millicent asked. 'Isn't there something about baked meats after a funeral? Or a funeral after baked meats?'

'I'm sure it doesn't apply to a parrot, Milly.'

'Why ever not? They are almost human. Too human sometimes.' She recalled the occasion when Isolde flew into the midst of some children who were shouting outside the Coppice. The children scattered, screaming.

'But I do have a lot to do for the fete, Maud.'

'It's all done except for the merry-go-round. Phil Appleby is fixing it.'

'And then there's—'

'You simply must come, Millicent. Where would I be without you?'

'Well, if you put it like that.'

'And that is exactly how I do put it. I will get your hat. The pretty floral one with, pardon me, the little bird. And why don't you change into something a little bit more graceful?'

'But I like this jumper.'

'You look a little *lumpen*, dear,' Maud said. 'It is Dorchester, after all.'

Millicent was persuaded to put on an outfit that she had bought at the Bargain Basement on Barnstaple high street. 'There now,' Maud said. 'Don't you feel pretty?'

'Are you sure this hat goes with it?'

'Like a horse and carriage.' For some reason Maud blushed. 'Doesn't she look pretty, Theo?'

Theo came out of his door as impeccably dressed as ever. 'She is a symphony in yellow.'

'More like a requiem.' Millicent was not to be soothed.

'We are a gay little party,' Theo said as they drove out of the Coppice. 'I feel like singing one of the songs from my old country.' Without clearing his throat, he began to croon: 'sei la mia stella, tu sei la donna che vorrei con me'.

'What is he singing?' Millicent whispered to Maud.

'Something about his star. That he would like to be with her. Oh God. I'm beginning to have my doubts.'

'Doubts about what?'

Maud did not reply at first. 'Life. Everything.'

On arriving in Dorchester Maud became more nervous as they turned into the car park of the town hall.

'Are we allowed to stay here?' she asked Theo. 'I think it is for the employees.'

'We will be permitted,' he replied. 'I will lead the way.'

They left the car and went up the steps to the main entrance. 'Goodness, this is grand,' Millicent said as they went through the double doors into the vestibule. 'It is more like Florence than Dorchester.'

Theo knew his way and took the two ladies down a series

of corridors until he stopped outside a door with 'Registry Office' inscribed in black and gold. 'Oh my goodness,' Millicent said, 'don't tell me we're going in here!'

'We wanted it to be a surprise,' Maud told her. 'Otherwise you might have cried. Here. Take this.' She took out of her handbag a packet of Uncle Ben's rice. 'Throw it all over us when we get outside. Not one by one, dear. But in a cluster. Like cold hail.'

On the drive home Millicent was too astonished to speak. Maud broke the silence.

'You must have guessed that something was going on.'

'I didn't know that anything was going on. I just thought we were all friends.'

'We *are* all friends. Friends are more friendly than ever. That's all.'

Millicent stared hard out of the window. Was Maud somehow her superior? Another thought appalled her. Would they move in together? And, worse, would they knock the two cottages into one? The thought of being able to hear their secret conversations was almost unendurable.

'Everything all right at the back?' Maud asked.

'Absolutely fine. I was just looking at the lovely laburnum across the street.'

'Ah yes,' Theo said, 'it is known in my country as the golden chain. But you must not touch it. It is poison.'

'Is that so?' Millicent was intrigued. 'Who would ever have thought it? It looks so peaceful. So pretty.'

The preparations for the summer fete were completed and, in a field just outside the village of Little Camborne, a variety of tents and stalls were erected. Maud Finch, who now insisted on being called Signora Cadmus, had been asked to preside over the lucky dip. Millicent Swallow was chosen to administer the teddy-bear tombola, and Theo Cadmus had agreed to look after a 'hand-made' stall that included a bottle made out of bamboo, a house fashioned from papier-mâché, and a pagoda made out of matchsticks. A stall for conserves stood in one corner of the field, together with another for potted plants. There was a coconut shy and a test-your-strength machine. A small ragtime band, its members complete with white blazers and straw boaters, had been recruited from a club of enthusiasts in Barnstaple.

The lucky dip and the hand-made stall were placed side by side, so that the new husband and wife could be seen by all the villagers. Above them was a banner, 'Signor and Signora Cadmus'.

'I don't think they should advertise the fact,' Jack Abbot said. 'It is not really English.'

'I want to get my palm read,' Signora Cadmus told her husband.

'Is that wise, carissima?'

'Why ever not? We've just been married. What can go wrong?'

A booth across the field bore the sign 'Mesmerical and Mystical Matilda. The Future Unfolds in the Palm of Your Hand.'

Matilda herself was draped in a tasselled shawl with a violet scarf around her neck. 'You're not from here, dear,' she told Maud. 'Some city or other. With water running through the middle. And there's a baby looming over you. Did you want to try the cards for a second look?'

'No thank you.' Maud rose to leave, depositing two pounds on the table. She left the tent and went back to her lucky dip. 'Nasty dirty gypsy,' she said to Theo and Millicent, 'spreading filth. She practically suggested I was pregnant.'

'You're meant to call them travellers, aren't you?' Millicent asked her.

'I don't care what you call them. She was a gypsy through and through. I didn't believe a word she said. A baby looming over me. Well, really. It's almost obscene.'

Some of the villagers were drifting from stall to stall, among them the deaconess. 'A little bird,' June said, 'tells me that I should congratulate you both.'

Theo smiled, turned around, and began talking to Millicent. 'Who was that little bird?' Maud asked her.

'No names. No pack drill.'

'Well, she – or he – may have been right.'

'I do wish it could have been in St Leonard's.'

'Theo is a Catholic.'

'But surely he could have stretched a point?'

'I'm afraid not. He is very devout.'

'But we could still have a service of thanksgiving?'

'Oh no. That really won't do. Theo has already pledged us to the Blessed Virgin Mary. In a private ceremony.'

'Oh dear,' June said. 'Is that wise?'

'Wise?'

'It is a little odd. It smacks of superstition.'

'You have to be odd to get married in the first place.'

'That's one way of looking at it.' June did not know how to reply.

'Think of me and Theo,' Maud smiled.

The ragtime band came around again, playing 'The Trouble I'm In'. A group of village chidren ran over to the tent, uncertain whether to try the lucky dip or the teddy-bear tombola.

'Horrible little things,' Maud muttered to Theo. 'Keep them away from me. I might bite.'

'What's in there?' A boy pointed to the lucky dip.

'Handcuffs. Mouse traps. Needles and pins. Poison. That sort of thing.'

The boy ran off, quickly followed by the others.

'What I would have liked,' a red-faced woman told Theo, 'is a bottle of home-made wine.'

'I can make wine,' Millicent called out from within her tent. 'Elderberry wine. At the end of the month, it will be everywhere.'

Theo seemed delighted at the prospect. 'Will you teach me, Milly? Back home, my limoncello was the best in the whole world.'

Millicent came out of her tent. 'We shall make it together, if Maud does not mind.'

'Not at all. It will give him something to do!' Then in a quieter tone Maud went back to complaining to Jennifer Pound. 'Yes, I hate this kind of thing. I am beginning to despise village life and all its horrible home-made wines. Whatever happened to candy floss?'

'Here it is!' Millicent called. 'Candy floss galore!'

'See?' Maud asked Jennifer. 'Everybody knows everybody's business. Even candy floss.'

'What an embarrassment of riches.' Sheila Burton pretended to view the stalls with admiration. 'Aren't I lucky? Shall I go for the hand-mades or for the lucky dip?'

'It's entirely up to you,' Maud said, in a voice that was not encouraging.

'I feel like plunging my hand into your tub, Maud.'

'Go ahead. You may get quite a surprise.'

'How exciting.'

Sheila put in her hand and began to rummage about in the wood shavings. 'Here!' she exclaimed. 'This may be some-thing wonderful.' She unwrapped it at once and found a bar of Cadbury's dark chocolate.

'Just the luck of the draw,' Maud said. 'That will be a pound. Try again.'

When Sheila stared excitedly into the depths of the sawdust, Maud looked at her in contempt. 'Do you see why I am sick of Little Camborne?' she asked Theo.

'But now we are settled here,' Theo replied.

'Oh, are we?'

'We love Little Camborne. We love our little house.' They had knocked an internal door through their respective cottages so that it seemed within to be a single dwelling with two staircases.

'Do we?'

'What are you saying, my dear Maud?'

'I am not sure if I'm saying anything.'

'You are not thinking ahead. How could we leave poor Milly?'

'I am quite sure she can look after herself.'

Millicent Swallow heard them, and began calling out for the teddy bear tombola. 'Who would like to own a teddy bear? A cute little teddy! A friend in good times and bad! Here's your chance to win one!' She came out of the tent. 'Now, Maud, I'm sure you'd like a nice cuddly companion.' At that moment came a piercing shriek from the merry-go-round.

The ragtime band ran off in panic, dropping their boaters in alarm.

Another shriek rang out. 'Hold the fort,' Maud told Theo as she rushed over to the source of the alarm. She found Sidney holding up something wrapped tightly in a blood-stained handkerchief. Maud touched it and pinched it. 'It's a finger,' she said. 'No, it's a thumb. Now what is a thumb doing here? Put it back on the merry-go-round in case you drop it.'

A police car quickly arrived, and Theo Cadmus noted with interest that the men were of higher rank than their predecessors who had investigated the robbery at the post office. At this instant the merry-go-round began to increase its speed. 'Phil Appleby is under there!' Maud cried out. 'He was fixing the screw bolts!'

As the machine gathered speed the inspector (as he turned out to be, to village amazement) dashed beneath the merry-go-round and after a few long minutes had pulled and half-dragged out the body of Phil Appleby, bleeding profusely from a thumb torn apart by some piece of machinery. He was unconscious and his brother, alerted to the accident, burst ino tears and lay on top of him.

'That is not the way to do it,' Cadmus whispered, and very gently lifted off Appleby's brother. 'Ambulance,' he called out but, as it transpired, one had already been summoned.

Sidney watched the severed thumb, swathed in a handkerchief, going round and round the outer rim of the merry-go-round at a slowly increasing speed until the policeman swooped upon it and retrieved it.

Chapter 17

Very Poorly

'To tell you the truth, I haven't been sleeping well since the tragedies. Is it true that poor Appleby bled to death?' Maud was confiding in the chemist on Barnstaple high street, Mr Lowe.

'His brother never got over the shock.'

'And to think that they served in the same squadron.'

'Platoon. You must get these things right, Maud.'

'I can get it right, thank you. There were six of them, I know that, although originally they were seventeen. Cunningham was still lieutenant, I suppose. Nobody tells us anything. Eleven of them were caught on a beach by the Germans. I don't know where. Was it France? Or Italy?'

'I thought it was New Zealand.'

'Oh dear, no. Far too far. But then there is the extraordinary thing. They all died here in England. In Devon, actually. It's been in the papers.'

'There are rumours, Maud. Of vengeance. By enemy aliens. They were supposed to have escaped from the POW camp in Crickley.'

'There are always rumours in Little Camborne. Who on earth would want revenge? It is not as if we had Germans here. They were all Poles, weren't they? Very hard-working. Ah, Theo. I was telling Mr Lowe that we have no trace of revenge here. The war is done.' Mr Cadmus had entered the shop and was examining the hair lotions.

'As far as I am aware, Maud.'

'So what do you recommend, Mr Lowe?' Maud was continuing her conversation with the chemist. 'One feels so dreary during the day. Sometimes I don't feel like doing anything. I sit down for a minute, and I wake up an hour later thinking of blood.'

'You don't actually see blood?'

'Of course not. I am not so lily-livered.'

'It might happen.'

'Then Little Camborne would be awash with blood.'

'You need those little iron pills, Miss Finch. The green ones. And try the blue ones, too.'

'Do you think?'

'Of course. There's nothing stronger than iron, is there?'

'Everybody recommends something different, blue or green. I really don't know what to do.'

On her return to her cottage, Maud found Millicent in the front garden. 'It's very warm for this time of year,' Maud said, 'don't you think?'

In fact the weather was distinctly cold, but Millicent smiled and nodded in agreement. 'You must get Theo to make you some more of that lovely elderberry wine.'

In fact Maud felt so warm that, on entering the cottage, she began to sweat. 'Dear oh dear,' she said to herself, 'I must sit down.'

Theo came from the neighbouring kitchen with a cup of tea. 'I thought I heard you. Here. Warm yourself up.'

'I'm quite warm enough already, Theo, thank you very much. I've got that prickly sensation. What do you call it? Prickly heat?' She held out her arm. 'Do you see those little red dots? They've just come on.'

'What you need,' he said, 'is a cool bath.'

'I always thought it was sinful to have a bath in the middle of the day.'

'Not at all. It is a restorative.'

'I'll try those tablets from Mr Lowe. Perhaps they will help. Let me see.' She opened her bag, and handed him the two bottles the chemist had prescribed. Theo looked at them briefly, and then put them in a sideboard drawer.

'Whatever did you do that for?'

'Do you want to poison yourself with these potions? All you need is fresh air and good food. And good wine.'

'But I have no appetite these days. And scarcely any sense of taste. Do you think I should see a doctor?' Maud seemed nervous.

'The witch Sheila? You might as well see a vet, for all the good it will do. Just put yourself in my hands, Maud. All will be well.'

He put her to bed, where she stayed for several days. He brought her hot drinks and soups, some of them prepared by Millicent, who prided herself on her mulligatawny and her split pea. 'There,' she said, 'that will bring some colour to your cheeks.' Yet Maud remained resolutely pale.

Mr Cadmus was optimistic. 'I have got this new recipe, Maud. Lots of red peppers to purge the blood.'

'Are you sure that's what I need? I do get stomach cramps in the night.'

'Of course. Cramps are a sign that you're not eating enough.'

He would come into her room in the morning, humming a tune, and find the sheets soaked in a yellow acrid sweat;

he told her that she was expelling the bad humours that had invaded her. When she urinated in the bed, he scolded her as if she were a baby and said nothing more about it. When she shivered he put his hands on her forehead and massaged it.

One morning she woke up feeling unaccountably better. 'Oh, Theo,' she said, 'let's go for a ride. Anywhere. I don't care.'

So they took off towards Rimington, where she might catch a glimpse of the sea. 'What is this village?' she asked as they drove through.

'We had a drink here about a month ago.'

'Did we?'

When they reached Sandbank itself, she was astonished. 'I don't remember these streets being so steep.'

'We have been here many times, Maud. The streets are always the same.'

'Are they? Did they not incline in the opposite direction? What did you say this place was called?'

On their way back she began to suffer from what she called 'palpitations'. Her hands began to tremble violently and she seemed to have something blocked in her throat. He stopped the car and declared: 'Do you know where we are going? We are going to the doctor.'

'Not to her.'

'She won't bite.'

'I'm not so sure about that.' So they drove into Barnstaple and to Sheila Burton's surgery in Castle Street; by good fortune they arrived just at the end of her consulting hours. 'Why, this is a surprise,' she said.

'It's a surprise to us.'

'There's nothing the matter with you, Mr Cadmus. But I can see that your wife—' She put her hand on Maud's wrist.

'The pulse is very weak.' She took out her stethoscope from the drawer of her desk. 'And the heartbeat is uneven. Are you regular?'

'I beg your pardon?'

'Bowel movements.'

'Not really. They come and go.'

'Are you eating?'

'Just a bit of soup.'

'If you will go into the next room, Mr Cadmus. I can examine your wife.'

Maud looked horrified at the suggestion, but Theo complied. The doctor came in fifteen minutes later, and closed the door behind her. 'I believe your wife is not at all well. She is suffering from anaemia. I can give her something for that. But she is also very agitated. She is worried about something, but she won't tell me anything about it.'

'Her memory is not as good as it was.'

'No, it's not that. Memory is a fluid thing. I think she fears harm.'

'Harm? In what way?'

'I don't know. It may be nothing at all.'

'How could it be anything? We live a quiet life here. The only things that bother us are foxes.'

'Oh yes. "The little foxes that spoil the vines."'

'I don't understand.'

'It's a quotation.'

'We have no enemies, doctor. We are quiet.'

'But can you ever be really quiet? Even here? Sometimes the country breeds more vices than the city.'

'I know it. I come from Italy.'

'So you understand exactly what I mean.'

Maud was calling out for Theo behind the closed door.

'Keep watch over her,' the doctor said. 'She needs your strength at the moment.'

'Have you considered,' Millicent asked Theo, 'if she is doing this to herself?' She had come round to her neighbours', just after he had put his wife to bed and given her a spoonful of the potion the doctor had prescribed for her.

'Good God, no. Whatever made you say that?'

'It just crossed my mind. Do you know if she's been drinking secretly?'

'Of course not. She only ever has the elderberry wine. And she can't get drunk on that.'

'It's not my place to say so, but people can do strange things. Even Maud.'

'You must explain better, dear Millicent.'

'Who knows what any one of us might be capable of?'

They looked at each other without blinking. 'It's not a subject—' he began to say.

'That you wish to dwell upon, Theo?'

'That I have ever thought about, Millicent.'

He climbed the stairs to his wife's bedroom. He found her asleep but her pale face was drenched in sweat while she shivered between the sheets. Her eyes opened, and for some seconds she stared at Theo without blinking. He stood quite still until her eyes closed again, and she resumed her fitful sleep. She muttered some words which meant nothing to him, among them 'saffron', 'salt' and 'watch'. At one moment she raised her hands into the air with an expression of horror. Then she fell into a deeper sleep.

Theo went down to Millicent. 'She is at peace now.'

'What?!'

'She is sleeping.'

'Oh, I thought you meant – never mind.'

'What is happening to her, Milly?'

'This is the mystery.'

'Like a book?'

'No, not like a book. She has had a difficult life, you know.'

'I don't want to know about it.' He had no reason to tell her that he had once overheard a conversation between the two women on the subject of Maud's forced abortion. 'What is past is gone.'

'But remorse and anxiety, Theo, can affect the health.'

'We all have things to hide.'

'But some people hide them better than others.'

'What do you mean, Millicent?'

'I don't know, but you should watch her.'

And this is what Theo did. He watched his wife closely, as she seemed better or worse day by day. Sometimes she smiled as the sun streamed through the bedroom window. Sometimes she sighed and put her hands up to her face. One afternoon Theo played Brahms's Second Symphony in the drawing room downstairs, loudly enough so that Maud could hear it. 'No. Please don't,' she said. 'For some reason I can't listen to music now.' She would try some dry bread and soup, but would often vomit them up a few moments later. She sipped at the elderberry wine, which now seemed to be her only nourishment. She was becoming increasingly frail. 'Would you like to sit in the garden?' Theo asked her.

'Could I sit in a chair?'

'Of course.'

'Then I will.' He helped her out of the bed, and only just saved her from falling onto the floor. He led her slowly down the stairs, as she clutched the banister, swaying slightly, and half-carried her into the garden. Millicent was looking at her through the front window, but quickly withdrew into the shadows of the room.

'Oh look,' Maud said. 'The azaleas are in bloom. Is it the right time? These days some things bloom early, and some things bloom late. Who can tell?' She stopped for a moment and put back her head. 'Do you know, I think the birds are singing in Latin. Is that possible? Oh, that wind. It frightens me. It seems to blow through me. I can't settle anywhere. Please take me inside, Theo.'

Sheila Burton visited her on the following morning, after receiving an anxious phone call from Theodore Cadmus.

'She is looking very poorly.' She stared very hard at her, and then put her face close to Maud's. Then she stepped back. 'Can I be indelicate? Well, believe it or not, she is dead.'

Chapter 18

Sad Case

'Someone should take her inside,' Millicent said. 'It's not right. What will the neighbours think?'

'What the neighbours think,' Cadmus said, 'is neither here nor there. We should be more concerned with the local doctors. Nobody likes a sudden death.'

News travelled fast in Little Camborne, and Mr Lowe hurried down the high street with his medical bag, which most older patients asumed to be to all intents and purposes empty. 'I have already notified the coroner. Open-and-shut case.'

'What is that case?' Cadmus asked him.

'Heart attack. As soon as I saw her − Miss Finch, that is − I saw the signs.'

'Did you notice the white bands around her fingers? Could that have been mycocardial infarction?'

'It all boils down to the same thing, Mr Cadmus. Trust us. We have different ways of working.'

An ambulance arrived at the Dorchester infirmary, gathering a small crowd as it went. Maud Finch was well-known in the area. There was silence when she was carried into the small accident and emergency ward, and when the swing doors were firmly shut the murmured conversation began.

'I'd never seen her so poorly,' Millicent said. 'Not even now she is dead.'

'The change comes over quickly,' Jennifer Pound told her. 'They lose pounds.'

'My brother didn't,' Mr Lowe remarked. 'He ballooned. The doctor put it down to—'

'We don't need all the details, Mr Lowe. Not in front of Millicent.'

The formalities lasted all afternoon, but the surprise was great when the doctor and coroner announced from the steps of the infirmary that an autopsy would need to be called.

There was no doubt about the matter. A middle-aged lady had died of unknown causes, having previously enjoyed good health. She had died comparatively quickly, too. The news provoked alarm and excitement in Little Camborne, where an unanticipated death was a rare event. No one knew what to make of it. Could it have been cancer? Jennifer Pound believed it to have been leukaemia that had killed Maud; she had looked so pale the last time she had seen her in church. Alfred Crozier suggested that Maud had picked up some mysterious virus on her recent visit to London. It was whispered by Mr and Mrs Watson that Theo Cadmus had not perhaps been as kind and as attentive a husband as he had appeared.

The autopsy was held on the following Friday morning in Barnstaple, where Maud's body had been taken to the local hospital for further investigation. Theo and Millicent were both allowed in, and seemed astonished when the hospital pathologist requested more time for his investigation as a result of 'irregularities'. They looked at one another in alarm. What could this mean? It did not take long to find out. A formal inquest was held in the county court ten days later, when the sergeant and two police surgeons confirmed that Maud had been killed by a process of arsenic poisoning that had continued for several weeks. Some grains of the substance were found in her liver, and small changes of pigment were observed about her neck; certain lesions were detected upon her skin, and, as Mr Cadmus had shrewdly observed, transverse white lines could be seen across her fingers. These familiar symptoms were then confirmed by tests upon her blood and hair. Maud Cadmus had been unlawfully killed.

Sally Ryan put down the telephone and ran from her flower shop to the fruiterer across the road. 'Have you heard? Maud was murdered! Poisoned!'

'What? That can't be right!'

'It isn't right, but it's true!' She put her hands around her neck. 'Just think, Tommy! A poisoner!'

At the same moment Simon Furlough, the local tobacconist, was observing Theo Cadmus and Millicent Swallow as they left the court. They were not talking and were staring straight ahead. One or two people had gathered by the steps to watch them leave but they, too, were silent. Millicent and Theo did not glance at them but walked over to the court-yard where his car was parked; when they returned to the Coppice they went into their separate cotttages without exchanging a word. Millicent opened her front door and entered the corridor; she leaned against it after she had closed it and said, to herself, 'Fuck.'

Even before the funeral, the whole of Little Camborne knew that Maud's will had been read and that she had left her entire estate to Theodore Cadmus, with a codicil in the name of Millicent Swallow. The congregation was watching him as he arrived at St Leonard's for the service, which prompted questions about the absence of Millicent. She arrived five minutes later, and took her seat in the opposite aisle. Both were dressed in formal mourning, which she had softened with a single row of pearls. They stared straight ahead throughout the service, not glancing to either side, and were careful to avoid one another as they eventually filed into the churchyard for the burial. No one seemed ready to approach them until Sheila Burton went up to Millicent and embraced her. Theo slowly walked up to his car and drove away alone. His departure seemed like a signal, since several parishioners now surrounded Millicent with their condolences. 'You can't have expected it,' she was told. 'It wasn't natural, was it?' The name of Theo was not mentioned. 'Was she in any pain at all?'

'I don't know. I don't think so. She was very confused.'

'She must have known what was going on.'

'Why should she? None of us knew. At least—'

'I'm surprised she went so fast. These things can drag on.'

Even as they were talking outside the church a police car drove up to the cottage which Theo had once shared with Maud. 'Well, hello sir!' A middle-aged man climbed out of the car. 'How glad I am to see you!'

'I beg your pardon?'

'I am Inspector Barrington.'

'Mr Theodore Cadmus. We met at the time of the unfortunate thumb.' He gave a little bow.

'That was an accident we will not forget, Mr Cadmus,' Barrington replied. 'It was a freak event, as I recall.'

'Would you care to come into the Coppice? I shared it with Maud, as you know.'

'I would welcome the opportunity, sir. I would relish it.'

Cadmus opened the door, and the inspector followed him into the front room; Barrington remained impassive, and it would have been dificult to determine how much he observed.

'I have just been to my wife's funeral. But of course you knew that already.'

'Oh, many condolences. This is the lady, I take it?' He went over to a framed photograph of the newly married couple on the mantelpiece. 'Sad case.'

'Is it a case, inspector?'

'Oh, very much so. Can I be frank?'

'Please do.'

'We are not looking for the hand of God here.'

'What has God got to do with it?'

'Nothing at all. Nothing whatsoever. That is exactly my point. We are looking for a human hand, Mr Cadmus. But whose?'

'Come, inspector. Shall we clear the air?'

'If you find it dusty, sir.'

'I find it dreary. You know I have been left everything in my wife's will. Is that so?'

'That seems to be correct, Mr Cadmus.'

'Now tell me this. Would I willingly watch her die for the sake of an old cottage and a few savings?'

'Rather more than a few.'

'The amount is no matter. It is inconceivable. Anyone who knows me will confirm that.'

'But I don't know you, Mr Cadmus. None of us do.'

'Shall we sit down?' They took chairs at a slight angle, so that they need not look directly at each other. 'What do you wish me to tell you? Theo Cadmus is open like a book.'

'Where are you from, Mr Cadmus?'

'I was born on the beautiful island of Sardinia, but my family left there when I was very young.'

'Someone told me you were raised on a tiny island.'

'Sheer gossip. We travelled to Naples, where we remained throughout the war. We kept our heads down. That is the phrase? I left school when I was fifteen, and found work with a firm who dealt in wheat. I became a clerk, so to speak, with my nose pressed to the stone. At the age of nineteeen I journeyed to Rome where, lo and behold, I became another clerk. In an accounting firm. I stayed there for eight years, where I learned my German and my English. Then I went on to Munich, where I prospered and was put in charge of the branch office. From there I went on to Berlin, where I remained until 1978. But my thoughts were always of England. I have always been a romantic lover of this country.'

'Had you ever been before?'

'Oh no.'

'Not immediately after the war?'

'As I said, I was in Naples. And then later in Rome.'

'Did you have any connection with the Germans during the war?'

'Of course not.'

'So why did you learn the language?'

'I wanted to leave Italy by all means possible. German and English seemed ideal. Arrivederci, Roma. Do you know of this song, inspector?'

'Why did you come to England?'

'As I said, I am a lover. I stayed in London for a while, where my nephew was opening his hotel. But all the time my thoughts were of Devon.'

'Why did you choose Little Camborne?'

'You will not believe me. I placed a pin in a local map.'

'That is remarkable. And did you hit upon this cottage?'

'Oh no. I went to an estate agent. Bradford's in Barnstaple.'

'So you had no previous acquaintance with Maud — with your late wife?'

'Not at all. She was a delightful surprise.'

'It was a short romance.'

'I do not need reminding.' Theodore gazed sorrowfully at the photograph.

'Before your marriage, I mean.'

'We had many interests in common.'

'Such as?'

'Birds. Music. Local history. You will laugh at this. Buried treasure.'

'Oh really? Did you find any?'

'Alas no. Just our buried hearts.'

'Had you previously known Millicent Swallow?'

'How could I have done?'

'I have no idea, sir. But the same ladies are living at Little Camborne. They had also worked in the same hospital in West London, I believe.'

'It would be a coincidence, to be sure, to know two ladies from the same institution. But I hardly knew her.'

'Did you know if they were from different parts of London?'

'I am afraid these niceties confuse me, inspector. I am a Greek peasant.'

'Not Sardinian?'

'Now you confuse me even more.'

Two days later Inspector Barrington knocked on the front door of Millicent Swallow.

'I was expecting you,' she said.

'How do you do, Miss Swallow? It is very good of you, it really is. What shall I call you?'

'Millicent, I suppose. I hate Milly.'

'Quite right. Silly Milly on the Dilly.'

'I beg your pardon?'

'I beg yours. Just a London song.'

'Are you a Londoner?'

'Acton. Half in and half out.'

'Just as you are now. Do come in.' The inspector followed her into the front room. 'Have you considered that someone else might have killed her?' Millicent peered at Barrington.

'Someone else?'

'I presume you still believe that Mr Cadmus—'

'Oh no. Dear me. I never jump to conclusions. I plod on.'

'So you have an open mind?' She was insistent.

'Wide open.'

'You see, inspector, I assumed Theo – Mr Cadmus – had done it. A lot of people around here do. But now I'm not so sure. It seems a little too obvious, if you know what I mean. And human nature is so mysterious. So unfathomable.'

'Deeps too dark to dwell in.'

'Precisely. Sometimes I don't even know what I am thinking. So how am I supposed to understand others?'

'Perhaps you aren't.'

'Do you think it possible that some people can do things without realising what they are doing?'

'You mean they just act without reflection?'

'Reflection doesn't come into it. This is on a different level. Instinct. Need. I don't know. Say I were to burn down a barn. And someone came up to me and said, "You have just burned down a house." What if I replied, "A house, so what?" And I walk away?'

'That is where the police get involved, Millicent.'

'What have the police got to do with it? There is no motive.'

'There is punishment.'

'I give you that. But if you don't feel guilty, punishment has no meaning. It is even more terrible.'

'You have a vivid imagination, Millicent.' She stared at him.

'I believe I do, inspector.'

Chapter 19

A Bed of Roses

On the following morning Inspector Barrington surprised Millicent with a second visit. She prepared two cups of tea and looked at him expectantly. 'Your Miss Finch is proving to be a mystery,' he said. 'She seems to have no past. No birth certificate. No baptismal entry. She only turns up in 1946.' The inspector watched Millicent for her reaction.

'War damage. There was terrible carnage of records.'

'She first saw the light, as it were, in St George's Hospital in Knightsbridge.'

'Oh really?'

'And then she went on to teach at an elementary school in South Kensington.'

'Is that so?'

'Here's the funny thing,' he continued. 'You were enrolled as a nurse at St George's Hospital in late 1945. You could have known her. You could have recommended her.'

'Oh, I don't think so. She wasn't on my ward.'

'Do you know how she got there?'

'I learned later. She had a troubled childhood, I think. Death was so common in those days. We need not enquire.'

'How did you meet?'

'At St Edmund's. The school in Kensington. I knew some of the staff there. We had a similar outlook on life.'

'What was that?'

'Light and easy. Laugh it off.'

'Is that when you started sharing a flat?' Millicent looked at him for moment. 'National census. 1961.'

'Amazing what you people can dig up. Yes. We became friends for life. And then about a few years ago we decided to move down here. Early retirement broadens the mind. Or so I am told.'

'It was an odd arrangement.'

'How so, inspector?'

'With a cottage between you both.'

'I told her that a house between will help to keep the peace. And so it proved.'

'Until Mr Cadmus turned up.'

'Well, that is a different story.'

'I should not be tellling you this, Miss Swallow, but your neighbour might not be all he seems.'

'Go on.' There was spittle on the side of her mouth.

'We have been making some enquiries.'

'I guessed as much. You do not often find an Italian popping up in the English countryside.'

'He was arrested for smuggling, just after the war. In Italy. But everyone was smuggling. So he did a clever thing. He made himself useful. Somehow or other he had taught himself English, and he got a job with the Allies in Rome. As a translator. He knew the right people, and he did a little bit of digging. There were lots of Italians who had dealt with the Nazis. And he made it his mission to find out their dirty little secrets. Hidden stashes of money. Exploitation of Jews. That sort of thing.'

'I can see this coming, inspector. He got involved in bribery and corruption. Is that it?'

'Precisely so, Miss Swallow. My word, you would have made a good policewoman.'

'I knew he had a way about him.'

'But that doesn't mean he killed Maud.'

Millicent turned to the window, and stared out at the lane. 'I might as well tell you. There's no point in covering it up. It's too late for that. And it may be that she drew the tragedy upon herself. Maud was my cousin, inspector.'

'But why conceal the relationship? It was perfectly harmless.'

'In those days there was talk of family groups running departments. There was no National Health Service, inspector, just groups of family practitioners who really all knew each other. So, being young and impressionable, we decided that we didn't really need them. Besides, we could help each other in the long run. And then this came in the post last week.'

She handed him an envelope addressed simply to 'Miss Swallow'. Inside was a piece of lined paper on which was scrawled in red biro 'SHE KILLED HER BABY'.

'This concerns Miss Finch?'

'I presume so.'

'What do you know of it?'

'Of course, as her cousin, I knew or suspected. But, inspector, I may now shock you.'

'By all means.'

'In the years of the war abortions and infanticides were relatively more common. They were never discussed, but everybody knew what was going on. Nobody wanted a German war baby.'

'So you and presumably your cousin disposed of it.'

'As I said, it was common practice.'

'You know it was an offence?'

'The prisons would have soon been packed.'

Barrington put the letter in the inside pocket of his jacket. 'How many people could have known of this?' Millicent asked him. 'How many gossips in Little Camborne?'

'The same thing was happening all over the country,' he said. 'To answer your question, half the village could have been told of this.'

'So a note could have been put through my door to cause mischief. To muddy the water.'

Millicent went to the window and looked over the front garden. 'If there is one thing I hate, inspector, it is deceit. Human deception is a terrible thing, don't you think? It has such terrible consequences. It can ruin people's lives.'

'But who is deceiving whom, Miss Swallow? Did I say that correctly?'

'Yes, you did. Nominative and accusative. Top marks.' She stopped, coughed, and stared straight ahead. 'It's all such a mess.'

When the regular autopsy, following the formal inquest, was covened, Maud Finch was the only subject. Inspector Barrington was called and testified that there was evidence of suicide but not evidence of foul play. Millicent Swallow and Theodore Cadmus offered evidence of precisely conficting nature and, to make matters more complicated, the tendency of their answers seemed to flow in opposite directions. Cadmus admitted that Maud Finch, his wife, was prone to suicidal thoughts; and had purchased a book on the subject. No such book was found. Millicent Swallow said that as long as she had known her, Maud had never uttered any such sentiments and was, indeed, unusually cheerful. Millicent Swallow under severe cross-examination also revealed that Maud Finch had indeed 'abandoned' her newly born baby, many years ago, but she did not know the details; she believed that it was to be adopted, but the trail could not be followed through the paperwork. Theodore Cadmus swore that he had never heard of such a thing. Millicent Swallow confessed that her cousin did know a great deal about poisonous roots and herbs, while Theodore Cadmus denied that his late wife had had any knowledge of poisons. Theodore Cadmus also testified that his wife had said 'I have had enough', while Millicent Swallow repeated Maud's hopes for 'a good spring'.

After the inquest was formally concluded they did not look at one another until they came outside in the company of the inspector.

'What are we to make of it?' Cadmus asked her.

'I think we must assent to it.'

'I suppose suicide is a possibility.'

'Quite certain of it,' Barrington added.

'But that is no reason why we should not be good neighbours, Millicent.'

'No reason at all, Theo.'

'I suggest that we do something about poor dear Maud.'

'What did you have in mind?'

'You know that she can never be buried in the churchyard?'

'Why ever not?'

'Suicide.' He drew his forefinger across his throat. 'She will have to be burned.'

'Like a witch?'

'No, no. In a crematorium. I have been told that there is one in Barnstaple. We will sprinkle her ashes. And we will build some sort of memorial. A statue. A flower garden.'

'I don't think a statue would be proper. Too Mediterranean, Theo, if I may say so. Perhaps a bed of roses by the Taw?'

'That would be delicious. What a tribute.'

'Pink was her favourite colour. As you must know.'

'Of course. We will create a field of pink! Maud's field. And what about Montmorency? He belonged to you, but she became very attached to him. She never had many friends.'

'We will bury him on the funeral pyre, Theo, as she would have wanted.'

'Do you know what happened to him?'

Millicent stared up at him. 'I think Maud lost interest in it. It happens, I believe. She lost interest in a lot of things. I think you'll find the old toy in a cardboard box in the attic. Well, what was the attic.'

'So that is where we must go.'

'No one has been up there for ages. Since it belonged to three cottages, it seemed like lost space. Do we dare?'

'I will be with you,' Barrington replied. 'You will never be out of my sight.'

Millicent and Cadmus were assailed by a rancid, musty smell as they opened the trap door and climbed the attic stairway. 'Mushrooms,' Cadmus said. 'Bad mushrooms. But what have we here?' He was the first to recognise that the effigy of Montmorency had been ripped to pieces and the red felt tongue of the dog had been cut in half.

'Look at these,' Milly said with an expression of horror. She was staring. 'No. Don't look.'

Over the attic floor were scattered photographs of relatives torn in half. Aunt Helen had half of her face missing. Mr and Mrs Finch were glued together in an obscene pose. St George's had been turned into a torture garden.

'Bad mushrooms and bad magic,' Cadmus said.

'May I?' Barrington asked. He climbed the ladder, and stopped on the top rung.

'It may seem to you to be unthinkable, inspector,' Millicent told him. 'But I think she planned to kill us all. She hated the lot of us.'

'How do you know, Millicent?' Theodore asked her.

'I could just tell. She was the type. As soon as I ever saw her she turned the evil eye.'

'But what type is that?'

'Oh,' Barrington said, 'the type that commits murder is a strong type, Mr Cadmus. A hard type. It does not delay. It does not waver. It is like adamant. As soon as it sees its opportunity, it strikes. That is my theory, at least.'

'That doesn't sound like Maud.'

'Nothing sounds like Maud,' Millicent added. 'That was her strength. But as soon as I saw her at the hospital she didn't seem right to me.'

'But you were friends, Milly.'

'It was a tangle, I admit.'

'Wherever you look in Little Camborne,' Theo said, 'you see tangles. They are more frequent than pebbles or shells.'

'Are you seeing tangles, Mr Cadmus, or planting them?'

'Can you explain, Mr Inspector?'

'Have you ever noticed the sign we have in this country? "No Thoroughfare"?'

'No. It is not known to me.'

'It should be. I must tell you something, sir. When you moved to Little Camborne, you came upon two very interesting ladies.'

Millicent and Theo were walking by the sea and on their way back she came upon a piece of worm-eaten wood that bore a passing resemblance to the Virgin and Child. It was too good an opportunity for Millicent and Theodore Cadmus. She eagerly held it up to the sky as soon as they had returned to Little Camborne, but in her haste she snagged her finger on a tiny nail embedded in the side of the Madonna. Her blood ran across the back of the Christ Child.

'Well, of all the accidents,' the inspector said, with a trace of satisfaction, 'that must be the most unfortunate.'

'It will wash off, won't it?'

'Hard to tell. The wood is very old.'

'Well,' Theo said, 'I suppose it adds to its authenticity.' He took the figurine into the kitchen, where he tried to wash off the blood under the tap. But the water seemed only to spread even wider the red stain. It now reached the plump arms of the infant even as he sought the embrace of his mother. Theo was in fact gazing at the image when he suddenly observed to Milly that 'We must pray for Maud's soul'.

'That's a very Catholic thing to do, Theo. Are you sure you don't want frankincense and myrrh?'

'No. A simple prayer said.'

'In the church?'

'No, not in that horror. In the garden.'

'And who would join us?'

'Sally. Jennifer. A few others. We don't want a full congregation trampling over the flowers.'

On the following Saturday a small group assembled in what was once Maud's back garden. By common consent Theo began the prayers among the roses. 'O Gracious Lord and Holy Mother of God, the Blessed Virgin Mary.' There were some glances. 'We pray you humbly to look down upon your departed servant, Maud Finch, who devoted her life to the poor children of London and the unfortunate people of this parish.' No one was quite sure where that description had come from.

Theo began to sing 'Ave Maria' but the others quickly changed it to 'Lead, Kindly Light'.

Over the next few days the figure of the Virgin and Child seemed to become bloodier still, the stain creeping across the Madonna's outstretched arm. Millicent believed that the peculiarly damp atmosphere of North Devon was responsible for the change. Theo was not so sure.

He was bent over the kitchen table, two evenings later, chopping some parsley with a small kitchen knife.

LET ME HELP YOU WITH THAT.

He heard the words distinctly, as clear as they could be; it was Maud's voice. He looked up quickly, but there was no one there. He resumed cutting the parsley, but his hand shook so badly that he cut his thumb. Had she spoken?

He went over to the window and looked out at the garden. He could see the sun setting behind the branches and foliage of the trees, and the shadow cast a dark shape.

The investigations in Little Camborne were thorough but inconclusive, and the evidence against Maud, although interesting, was not proven. There was no evidence of foul play, either, in the sudden deaths of the soldiers. If there had been, it must have been very carefully disguised. But the villagers did not stop their rumours. Maud was cremated together with Montmorency, and the three back gardens dedicated to her and her dog. But the suspicions against Millicent and Theo did not abate.

Chapter 20

Enough Is Enough

'Well, I think, Milly, the time has come for a holiday. Enough is enough.'

'Is it not a little premature, Theo? Maud has just passed away.'

'Not if we concentrate our minds on amethysts. Everything points in that direction. The legends of the sea. The jewel in the rock. The stories of hidden treasure. The hikers on their trail. And the soldiers with their so-called booty.'

'None of it really amounts to much, Theo. And in any case this is supposed to be a holiday. Do you know what you are suggesting?'

'Of course. I am suggesting Caldera. Courage! Advance!'

'Oh dear. I was thinking of Eastbourne.'

'Where is the treasure in Eastbourne, Milly? You cannot deny me my mission.'

This clinched the argument, despite Milly's misgivings about this desolate island on the Tyrrhenian Sea.

'We will not need an atlas or globe. It is in my head. For you it will be pure pleasure.' Milly was not entirely convinced by his confidence.

'For the sake of company, can we invite Sidney to go with us?' she asked. 'He loves the sea. He was once a diver. Or so he tells me. And did you know that Tony—'

'Your wicked priest?'

'Vicar, actually. He is on the island. Jennifer Pound told me. No parish would take him. Not a surprise.'

'What is he doing there?' Theo asked.

'Making converts, I suppose.'

'Among the goats? Not at all. They are manifest pagans. Have you seen their horns? He will have more worldly concerns. He will know the stories of the amethysts.'

Caldera Air, by which they chose to fly, was a small and somewhat uncomfortable plane stocked with spirits and a number of 'snacks' that seem to have been manufactured in Dresden. 'The aeroplane satisfies every need!' Cadmus told her. 'The four hours will literally fly by.'

'Four hours!' Milly muttered.

In these four hours the heat in the airport at Sicily grew immense, but Cadmus was already gazing at the posters of the blue sea as their small aircraft docked by the departures lounge. Two or three small boats, with pennants waving, were waiting for them.

Cadmus, Sidney and Millicent made their way to Caldera in the first boat. It had dropped anchor in the bay beside the escarpment of rock where, as a boy, Theo had hidden after the explosion which killed his brother. In honour of his family he had staked out a claim to the shallow waters close to his old farmhouse and had constructed a pier across the adjacent sands and waters. It was the custom of the island to preserve territory in that way, and the space marked out as inalienable. They hired a farmhouse at an exorbitant price and in the following week, Theo also hired a boat to sail around the island noticing the small crags and inlets that he had once known so well.

Sidney took charge of the boat with great ease, and soon knew the tides and rivulets that swirled around the island. He had also heard stories of the amethysts for which the islands were famous and was determined to seek them out. On this bright morning, however, there came a splutter from beneath the boat, followed by a cough and what seemed a clearing of the throat. The engine fell silent.

'Oh, Theo!' Milly shouted. 'What is the matter?'

'A minor inconvenience, Milly dear. Look. We have Sidney with us. And here is our island salvation.'

Around the inlet came a small boat piloted by a young boy who had hired the craft to Theo, but was not at all sure of Sidney's sea skills. He had come to check the strange young man's sea-worthiness. Theo knew the boy's accent and began to explain their situation.

'Andiamo la . . . gli occhi viola.' The boy crossed himself. 'Il sequiranno.'

'Occhi viola. Now we come to the heart of the matter. These purple eyes are interesting, young man. Questi occhi viola sono interessanti.'

'Interessanti? No. No. Lasciamoli stare!'

Theo turned to Milly. 'You see the islanders are very primitive.'

He crouched before the boy. 'Ragazzo mio. Caldera e la mia isola. Occhi viola non possono farci male. Do you comprehend me? This is my territory. By right of family. And these violet eyes belong to me. They can do no possible harm.'

'This is the problem,' Sidney explained to Milly. 'One of the islanders has explained it to me. The water is cursed by sea witches and demons with purple eyes. The boy is afraid to enter it.'

Theo sighed, lay down in the boat and stared up at the deep blue sky. 'What can you do with savages?' Then he stood up. 'Occhi viola,' he said to himself. 'Purple eyes. What can they signify? Let me think.' With one nimble move he leaped to the other side of the boat, and imitated a rolling motion over the side. 'Can you dive like this?' he asked the boy. 'Puoi tuffarti così?'

'Si, certo.' He nodded vigorously to convey his assent in any language.

Theo took him to the side of the boat and engaged him in a conversation that Milly could not decipher, but from his gestures and expressions it obviously concerned money. Cadmus knew that even the superstitions of the people were soothed by coin. He was naturally concerned with the amethysts that were presumed to lie on the sea bed around Caldera. Theo had known of them since boyhood, but had once treated them with superstitious reverence in the same way as the other islanders. Some of the jewels were embedded in the rocks while others had spilled from wrecked galleons centuries before. But in this island region the amethyst was still sacred. Its purple was believed to be the most lustrous and deepest violet and the essence of the sea. As Theo put it to the boy, 'l più intenso e brillante in assoluto e esprimesse l'essenza del mare.' Such was their abundance, however, that some were green, or blue, or even red.

They came back day after day for a week, while Sidney explored the crags and headlands for suitable diving places. Milly continually warned him about the peril of tides and currents, but he showed her his compass and explored further afield. The third day he ventured out and did not return. The legend of the amethysts now took an ominous turn. The islanders believed that anyone who broke the geodes and took the jewels would incur the wrath of the lightning god who protected the stones; the amethysts would then in some way destroy the thief. It was an absurd story, but it was implicitly believed. Meanwhile Sidney, despite several searches, had not been found.

This superstition followed the members of the previous platoon who had died in quick succession in Little Camborne. It followed Maud Finch, who was popularly believed to own an amethyst brooch given to her by Theo as a wedding gift. The death of Phil Appleby was attributed to the small amethyst ring he wore on his thumb, which Theo had given him as payment for repairing his garden fence. This was the digit torn off by the merry-go-round. Then on the seventh day the Italian boy surfaced swiftly with a curious cry.

'Here is the man,' he shouted. 'It is Siderney! Siderney!' When the police boat arrived, and the corpse carefully brought to the surface, it was unmistakably that of Sidney. His death was quite out of the ordinary, however, since his mouth and nostrils were stuffed with green amethysts so that he could no longer breathe. Old stories were given fresh encouragement, and soon circulated around the island.

There was, for example, the legend of the green microscope. One revered physician, Doctor Rhadamantus had dwelled on the island for all of his life, and had made an especial study of the rare stones that washed over the beach. There were often tumults beneath the ocean, which were widely believed to be the residue of volcanic eruptions. This part of the sea was in fact well known to geologists for seismic interruptions, although the islanders called them by different names.

This physician was walking along the strand one quiet evening, some years ago, when he saw a sparkle in the sand – not a sparkle of sunlight but a glinting blue ray. He had read of amethysts to be found under the adjacent sea, but this particular stone caught his attention. It was warm to the touch, and when he put it to his ear he could sense the pounding of the waves. This was unusual enough to provoke his curiosity, and he held the fragment up to the sky. How could this be? The sky had become dark, and the clouds blood-red. When he then looked through the amethyst at the sea, it was as pale as milk, and peculiar creatures seemed to frolic in the foam. Rhadamantus maintained his composure, having listened to many anedcotes about the jewels, and speculated on the nature of the primaeval stone. There was no doubt that it was primordial. But how could it reflect strange images? It was a curious feature of the island that extravagant speculations were entertained side by side with primitive beliefs. The doctor rubbed and polished the green stone so that he could see no flaw in it, and when he put his eye up to it he was astonished by the multitude of stars reflected within it. They seemed to form spiral nebulae and regions of darkness spinning across the dark sky. He was so entranced that he was not at all sure where he was walking, and this was the origin of the legend that Doctor Rhadamantus had been lured by an amethyst over the cliff.

Another story of the amethyst was widely carried over the island in connection with a purple seagull. Sometime at the beginning of the last century a colony of gulls settled in the fissure between two sheer cliffs. The competition between them for food was intense, and any rare specimen was taken before any competitor could appear. On this occasion a roving gull caught a glimpse of what looked like a green egg, harbouring what delicacy? The gull carried it off to a hollow in the cliff where not even the keenest gull could spy it, and covered it with sticks and straw. But the egg seemed strangely quiet. It did not respond to the mature bird's murmurings but instead, when it was broken open by the gull's beak, the hatchling let out a strange sibilant hiss. And it was purple. On a small island this odd bird caused some sensation, and efforts were made to catch it. But it eluded capture, and seemed to take joy in pursuit and disappearance. It appeared in the oddest places, and seemed not to touch the diet of the ordinary gull. The islanders soon knew all about it, and young Theo tried without success to track it down.

Then there was another extraordinary development. According to the records kept by the Capuchin monks of a neighbouring island the bird grew and grew in height and stature until it was twice the size of the ordinary bird and had turned a deeper purple. There followed a further misadventure. The bird had kept aloof from its companions and professed disinterest for them; but then at about twilight on 4 May 1936 a sound of screaming and screeching alerted the inhabitants of Caldera. They rushed into their gardens, where the birds were kept in cages, and to their horror found the great green bird tearing and eviscerating its companions; how it had forced its way through the bars of the cages was not at all clear; but the islanders were more than ever convinced that it had supernatural powers.

The bird did not leave Caldera. It settled, and gave every attempt to control the other birds with a series of squawks and flourishes of its feathers. Some believed that the war had affected them and that the noise of bombs and shrapnel had rendered them delirious. But this seemed to be too strange a fear. A group of islanders solemnly carried a black cloth into the garden and draped it across the green bird's nest. The creature made no noise. They carried it up to to Pilot Cliff, the highest point of all, and then without more words hurled it into the rocks and sea. It issued one piercing cry and somehow escaped the folds of the cloth. When it reappeared on the surface of the water, bobbing on the waves, the islanders were thrown into confusion and a certain amount of fear. Some of them fled the cliff-top, and took refuge among the tall grasses while above them the green bird took flight, and issued its sibilant murmur.

Chapter 21

In My Head

The death of Sidney had given Millicent what she called 'the shakes'. Sensing her mood, Cadmus suggested an expedition around Caldera as a diversion. A small party of boats, hired by tourists visiting Sicily, had beached on the shore and Theo had agreed to assist their guide. 'Now, ladies and gentlemen,' he said, 'we will begin our climb. As I told you, the path is still here. It will not be difficult. It will be easy!'

Theo knew where they were going. They were advancing upwards, brushing past the cliffs, to the highest part of the island close to the tower where he had been assaulted by the Englishman. It scarcely seemed possible that he had returned. He closed his eyes, and felt the same sun upon his face; the bees hummed, and the long grass touched his legs.

And here was the tower itself, still the colour of moss and earth.

'Let's go up,' Milly said.

'Oh no, it is too old. It will be dangerous.' Theo looked to the tourists' guide for confirmation.

'Nonsense,' she replied. 'It is made of good stone.'

'Stone crumbles.'

He crossed the threshold and looked up uncertainly at the winding staircase. He smelt something putrefying in the heat.

'You look as if you have seen a ghost,' Milly said.

'Oh no, I've never been here before.'

'That's a funny answer,' the guide remarked.

'I mean, I have no reason to see anything.'

'Come on, Theo.' Millicent took the lead in climbing the stairs until they reached the open space at the top, where the Englishmen had confronted the boy Cadmus. 'Well,' she said. 'I see no ghosts.'

'I told you,' Theo said. 'There is none to be found here. This is just an old and rotting building.' He went over to the arched recess that looked out towards the Tyrrhenian Sea. 'If there is a chill in the air,' he said, 'it comes from the sea wind.'

As the party began its descent Cadmus passed the part of the forest where he had directed the English soldiers to the dying German. He could not make out the precise spot where the man had lain. But he hastened ahead, telling Millicent that she should hurry away with the others because such a place was a haven for snakes. On their way back to the boat he caught a glimpse of the ruin that had once been the farmhouse where he had lived with his parents and his brother. It still stood. He lingered on the old ground while the tourists ventured onto the boat.

'We must catch up with the others,' Milly said, sensing his unhappiness. Much to her surprise he knelt down and kissed the ground. 'Whatever next?' Milly asked him. 'We are Episcopalians, not Papists!'

'You may be. But I am Calderian!'

'Oh, I suppose you have become a disciple of the reverend Tony.'

'There is no need for blasphemy, Milly.'

It was quite by chance that a few days later Milly encoun-
tered the reverend in the marketplace of Olba, on the eastern
part of Caldera, fingering some silver crucifixes. 'I had heard
that you had come here,' she said. 'But no one could give me
a reason.'

'One reason lies before you. Silver is cheap here, compared
to the notorious amethysts.' At first he did not seem to
remember her name. 'No offence!' he said.

'None taken.'

'Quits?'

She was not sure what he meant but she accepted the
compliment with which it was offered.

'I know you had the best of intentions, reverend, rescuing
the church treasures from the heathen, but don't you think
you should make yourself known to the authorities?'

'What did the Lord say, Miss—'

'Swallow.'

'There is no authority above the Lord our God, Miss
Swallow. Praise him for ever and ever. Pay what belongs to
Caesar and withold what belongs to Belial.'

'Quite.' She was not sure what he meant.

'Naturally, I was very sorry to hear that Sidney had been
taken up by a higher power.'

'That was a terrible shock,' Millicent said. 'I practically
broke down. But I took some honey and rallied.'

'Did he say something? Anything?'

'Not as far as I am aware.' There was a look of relief on
the reverend's face.

'But the heathen is still here,' he told her.

'Oh?'

'I speak of your friend, Theodore Cadmus. He has set
himself up as an expert. He has a mass of jewels.'

'The amethysts?'

'Of course. But you have to know where to find them.'

'And I presume that Theo does?'

'He has made a special study of them. Between you and me, that is why he returned to Caldera.'

'Is that so? I can tell you something else. Maud told me all about it after she married him. She dropped her voice to a whisper – 'he really wanted Sidney. If you know what I mean.'

'Curiouser and curiouser.'

'Of course we can't prove any of this.'

'Not unless—'

'What?'

'Unless you confronted him,' he said. 'As his especial confidante.'

'He would rather cut out his tongue.'

'Perhaps I can help you. As the minister here.'

'Tony, may I speak frankly to you?'

'You may speak as you so desire.'

'I have been speaking to the people who own our farmhouse. The islanders do not consider you as minister of anything. They wish you to be gone.'

'Tell them not to be concerned. I will be gone as soon as I can. Between you and me, I have accumulated some amethysts of my own.'

'But surely they belong to the island?'

'It is not *the island's* collection. It is nobody's collection. It is the collection of the sea and the waves and the foam and the sands of time.'

'But what about the islanders?'

'Savages.'

'But aren't the jewels still private property?'

Tony laughed. 'Tell me what is private here? The echo from the caves? The snow on the peaks? The serpents on the beach?

A lot of it is nonsense. Cadmus nonsense. But he is correct in one particular. There is a rare species of purple bird that flourishes here. And they have a strange affinity with the geodes and amethysts. When you find the birds, you find the jewels. I can see that this interests you.'

'It is intriguing. But why should I not ask Theo's help in finding them? He likes to think of himself as king of the island.'

So Tony and Milly decided that, with the help of Cadmus, they would begin a survey of the island by close questioning of the islanders, and it soon became apparent that there had now grown up a myriad of great purple birds, each with the same sibilant murmur and the same sequence of nesting places.

Cadmus already knew where to locate the usual song of the original purple bird, since after its capture it had returned to the same arbour. He had found some primitive recording equipment in an abandoned hospital in the middle of the island, and surreptitiously taped its peculiar call. This had been the reason for his success. Cadmus now agreed to assist them, promising himself that they were amateurs and that their efforts would amount to very little.

So the three of them, two days later, made their way to some evergreen oaks pressed close by cork oak trees, resembling a skull, where Cadmus believed the bird nested. Eventually it burst into melody in response to the taped song, and at that instant Cadmus took out an axe from his backpack and split the tree down the middle. The bird uttered a ferocious scream as a stream of purple stones cascaded from the wood. It launched an attack upon Cadmus, at which he yelled and ran down the hill. Tony and Milly, of more phlegmatic temperament, remained quite still and waited.

'We are mad to stay here,' Tony told her.

'There is a method to it, dear Tony. Did you notice that Cadmus, despite his fear, ran down a particular path to a particular hollow?'

'I was too distracted.'

'But Cadmus was not so distracted. He has his eyes open for the prize.'

'You mean?'

'He thinks he knows the path to the jewels.'

'I wish I had your brain, Milly.'

'Be very careful what you wish for, Tony. Is that not the phrase?'

They followed the track that Cadmus had taken, descending further into dense vegetation. Tony had a fear of insects, and uttered a series of screams and yelps. They entered a cave plastered and decorated with florid iridescent feathers, one of which resembled a head-dress.

'If I remember,' Milly said, 'Milton describes a region of sub-aqueous fire. I hope he was wrong.' Tony did not know what she meant, and tried to concentrate upon the feathers that decorated the cave among the trees.

'Now here is a question,' Milly said. 'Were the decorations made by men or birds?'

This alarmed them, for reasons which they did not wish to fathom. It occurred to Tony that they were entering some pagan domain, but the consequences were too frightful to contemplate. 'Cadmus knew where he was going,' Milly told him. 'He simply disappeared from sight.'

This alarmed Tony further. 'How far down do we have to go?'

'To the bottom,' Milly replied.

'Oh my God. And what if we can't get up again?'

'Follow the track of Cadmus. But be quick about it. He is elusive.'

They proceeded in silence, acutely conscious that the great green birds were watching and listening. They came to level ground sooner than they expected, and found Cadmus staring at the roof of the cave. An odd squawk, magnified in the confined space, alarmed Tony and he grabbed Cadmus's arm; but, more alarming still, it was succeeded by what Tony believed to be quiet laughter. 'Did you hear that?' he asked Cadmus. 'It sounded like you.'

'The birds are good mimics.'

'So they must have been listening to you,' Milly said.

Tony tried to regain his composure, but he cried out when he glimpsed the shadow of feathers against the wall of the cave together with a rustling sound. 'There *is* something in here,' he said.

'Perhaps it would be better,' Milly said, 'if we tip-toed away.'

The already jewel-encrusted corpse of Sidney was guarded by iron gates in the village cemetery. It was believed that the curse of the amethyst had manifested itself once again, and the temperature of the island seemed perceptibly to be lowered. *Giornale di Sicilia* reported that the children had become listless and irritable, while the adult population crammed into a little church where the reverend Tony felt himself finally to be respected. The incident of the burglary was now conceived to be a bad omen, which no one could have foreseen. It was believed that Sidney was what the police would have called 'una persona di interesse' but his corpse put the matter to rest. It seemed, in fact, that the expedition had come to an end. Other travellers – Theodore, Milly and Tony among them – began the slow removal to Little Camborne.

Chapter 22

The Funeral

But this resolution did not satisfy the reverend Tony, who still meditated upon the overgrown path that Cadmus took into the cave. Why had he sought the winding and treacherous rock outcrop with its snakes and insects when a perfectly even lane would have led him in the same direction? The reverend, too, had caught a glimpse of the feathered head-dress as a shadow in the cave, and recalled the laughter as an apparent imitation of Cadmus's voice. He had a suspicion that it was a hallucination, magnified by the cavernous rocks and crevices when shadows become real objects and stray noises become audible voices; he had become aware of similar phenomena in Lesser Guinea. He now became all the more convinced when images of a feathered creature with a serpent's tail seemed to glide along the walls of the cave; he was for a moment close to panic until he realised that they were striations created by the rising light.

There was only one possible solution to the discovery of the jewels – to follow Cadmus's trail as closely as could be and mark the signs that he followed. It was only two days before their departure. Tony did not expect to obtain any help from the islanders, especially after Milly's warning that he was not welcome. He set out just before dawn in the still cool air, and soon found a scruffy unkempt path which seemed to trace circles in the terrain before bounding back on its self. This was the one.

Or was it? He followed it closely for more than a mile and could find no clue to its eventual direction except that it wound steadily downward. A few marks in red ochre meant nothing to him, except as signs of human intervention, but they were enough for him to persevere. Then he came across a dislocated jaw bone of a small monkey with something glistening as the sun rose above it. It was an amethyst. He had found the way. With redoubled step he hurried down the path, when he heard the echo of footsteps not his own. 'I am the reverend Tony,' he called. 'There is no need to hide from me. I am all friend.'

A familiar figure stepped out of the shadows. 'Good morning, friend. I knew that you would return, And voila! You find Theo Cadmus with the greatest of ease. He is your greatest supporter on the island!'

'Supporter?'

'This is not a Christian country. Far from it. You need protection.'

'That is not very reassuring.'

'And if the island is not Christian it does not obey Christian precepts. Is that so? You must ask your parishioners, if you have any. Adultery. Bigamy. Murder, perhaps? Anything is possible.'

Theo took his arm and walked with Tony from the cave towards the steep incline that led to the top of Pilot Cliff. 'The vista is disturbing, is it not?'

'Not if you were disturbed already,' Tony replied.

'So the seascape imitates the inhabitants. An interesting idea.'

A loud rumble of thunder came from the direction of Punta La Memora, and across the island the elderly population crossed themselves. It was a warning.

'Bad sign. We must go beneath the ground,' Theo said. 'It will save us from any harm.'

He took the sleeve of Tony's jacket, and dragged him into the smallest cave visible.

'We are safe. Here we cannot be found.'

Tony had no idea what he meant but felt his familiar panic in caves. He looked in horror at Theo, who was smiling broadly at him.

Theo pushed him into the depth of the little cave and then, with remarkably little fuss, brought out a long knife with which he sliced Tony's breast bone. Tony made no cry but a soft drawn-out sigh.

'Is this it?' he whispered.

'For sacrilege,' Theo told him. 'For desecration. For blasphemy. You are on a sacred island protected by immortal birds. It is a pity nobody told you. But ignorance is no defence—'

He stopped as a gush of blood came out of Tony's side. He spat at the enlarging pool. 'Caldera is older than Christianity. The minister should know that. Ignorantia juris non excusat. That is the phrase, reverend.' And at that moment he took out the dagger and thrust it through Tony's belly.

The disappearance of the minister did not cause much consternation. Prelates often visited the island, and were known to make hasty departures; it was not considered a healthy community by any Christian standard. Talk of blood sacrifices and burials at sea had been the general gossip of many years, and the apparent friendliness of the islanders was believed to be a cover for deviousness and deception. It was widely surmised, for example, that before Theodore Cadmus left for England he had been the guardian leader of the Calderian sect that exercised a considerable martial and social authority over the adjacent islands. Everybody knew of his wartime exploits with the German and English soldiers but few chose to discuss them.

The geology of the island had become more precarious after the loud thunder, and the islanders grew ever more fearful. There were several violent explosions or gusts of scalding air which issued from the already unstable earth. Streams of molten amethyst then burst into the air. The green jungle turned grey and dry, and pillars of molten and semi-molten quartz spread over the island.

There was a further surprise. The priest on the cemetery island of Nacoro, who buried the bodies of the islanders, and who had buried Theo's parents many years before, was found lying in an unmarked grave alongside the fisherman who had been the grave-digger. Theirs were not the only corpses to be discovered on the island, which soon became known as 'The Fatal Isle of Amethyst' or more dramatically 'The Reliquary of Death'.

Later in the same month occurred one of those inexplicable events which has its origin in the depths of the earth. It had been widely reported that there had been sporadic eruptions of molten amethyst for several years, which had been explained as random fissures in the earth's surface. Specimens were taken to the Geological Museum in Cagliari – which was essentially an amethyst museum – where no particular aberrations were discovered. There were cracks and splinters but nothing unusual. In March some tremors were perceptible, but they subsided as quickly as they arose. At the beginning of April, however, an enormous crack was felt and heard throughout the island. It had all the characteristics of an earthquake, and at once the islanders took to their boats and ships and small craft in fear of the deluge to come. Milly and Theo were among them, hiring an islander to take them and their luggage to Sicily and the airport.

But the principal danger came from fire and not water. The earth gave way in many places, opening holes and fissures through which the amethyst gushed forth and covered the local terrain. Such was the power and velocity of the quartz rock that it poured upon the hills and valleys of Caldera, destroying everything it touched. All those who were caught in its apparently endless flow were instantly petrified by its power so that they seemed to be carved out of amethyst. Pillars of amethyst burst out from the earth like glittering shafts so that for a moment they resembled Greek temples trembling in the unaccustomed light. One of the investigators found the leaf of a rose, entirely encased in purple stone, lying on the floor beside a pew. But of course it had no scent; the perfume of the thyme, the heath and the rosemary, so redolent of the island, had entirely disappeared. The Cadmus farmhouse barely stood, but there were remnants of a stove and olive press and, curiously enough, part of a cuckoo clock.

The statues, or petrified forms, had in fact been entombed in amethyst, ash, pumice and plaster so that the configurations of their bodies were imprecise. An archaeological team from the mainland discovered one hundred and fifty bodies, including pregnant women as well as a mother and child in their final moments. A face lay on a pillow, strangely quiet; fierce fires broke out but they were cooled or dampened by great grey clouds coming across the sea. The first bodies had been found among the remains of the cemetery island of

Nacoro, the bodies laid beside each other. They were not anonymous; their costume had not faded completely and the jewellery – including many amethysts – were, after polishing, still bright.

Chapter 23

The Aftermath

On the morning of their sudden return from Caldera to Little Camborne Theodore Cadmus went down into the kitchen and prepared a pot of tea; he poured three tablespoons of sugar in it, which he had never done before, and sat outside in the back garden. 'You're looking well,' Millicent said, as she came out into her own garden. 'Nice colour on your cheeks. It's a lovely morning.'

'Yes, isn't it?'

'I see you started work early.'

'What?'

She pointed to a patch of freshly dug earth between two rose bushes.

'I had nothing to do with it. There is no space. They will be packed like the sardines.'

THERE IS ROOM I THINK BUT ONLY IF YOU ARE CAREFUL.

'I beg your pardon, Milly?' Cadmus asked.

'I didn't say anything.' But then he heard this distinctly from Maud —

I WOULD LEAVE IT BE.

Millicent did not hear this remark, but Cadmus heard it as clearly as Maud Finch's voice. 'Don't you think Maud would have loved our rose garden?' Millicent asked him. 'She might have planted it herself.'

AND WHO ELSE COULD HAVE DONE IT? THE PARROT? The spirit of Maud seemed to be losing her temper.

'Do you remember how you dreamed of a rose tree, Theo, and it blossomed overnight? It seemed to be conjured up by a spirit.'

WARMER.

'Sometimes I am led to that conclusion, Milly. I am sure there is a phantom here who likes to imitate Maud. We have such beings on Caldera. We call them spettri.'

'You still have ghosts on your mind, Theo. It isn't natural.'

'Think about it, Milly. A platoon of six soldiers dead. Peculiar deaths, not least on the funfair. Sidney drowned among amethysts. My poor island devastated by earthquake. You can hardly call this natural.'

They sat down to tea. 'Why have you laid three cups and three plates?' Milly asked him. 'Or is that also supernatural?'

'Force of circumstance. I've been meaning to tell you that I hear—'

A WASTE OF WASHING UP.

'Milly, have you not heard voices? Like that one?'

'Like which one? Saying what?'

'Oh. "I CAN HELP YOU WITH THAT" and "I WOULD LEAVE IT BE". Silly words like that.'

'What nonsense, Theo.'

'But I hear them all the time. And have you noticed that there are three glasses and three toothbrushes in the bathroom sink?'

'Rubbish.'

The spectre of Maud had lost her temper.

OH REALLY. AND HOW DO YOU EXPLAIN THE EARTHQUAKE? ASK THEO WHO TAUGHT MILLICENT TO MAKE ELDERBERRY WINE. THAT WAS WHAT KILLED ME. THEY PLANNED IT. THEY WANTED THE COTTAGE. I COULD TELL YOU WHERE ALL THEO'S JEWELS ARE BURIED BUT I REALLY CAN'T BE BOTHERED. ALL I CAN DO IS HELP TO BURY THE PAST.

At that juncture the messages were lost to Theo's ears. Millicent had heard nothing at all, but was slightly puzzled by Theo's placid smile.

He had the same smile on his face when, one late May morning, he was found lying dead, beneath the rose tree in what had once been Maud's garden. By late summer the roses were ready to bloom and the Coppice became well known for its deep roseate hue. It was considered by some to resemble a living amethyst.